Murder or Justice

D M Gaines

New Flavor

Books

Murder or Justice

Editing and cover design by
Earvin Taze Watters Jr.
ezatcreations@yahoo.com

Visit our website: Newflavorsbooksandpublishingllc.com
New Flavor an imprint of New Flavor Books & Publishing, LLC

New Flavor Books & Publishing, LLC
PO Box 603323
Cleveland, Ohio 44103

This book is dedicated to all of the parents, who fight their best to keep their children safe from the evil that lurks in the streets.

Books by D M Gaines

Hood to Hood: A Cleveland Story
Hood to Hood 2: Spank's Revenge
Sexual Addiction: Director's Cut
All Flavors: A Book of Erotic Short Stories
Bisexual Bliss
Hitting' Licks
Murder or Justice
Deadly Surgeon

I would like to give thanks to my best friend since childhood Darrin Fears. You are the only true friend that I have ever known. I would like to thank my daughter in law Beverly Johnson. Thank you for all of your help. And thanks to everyone out there, who supports me. May you all be blessed Thanks to the following people from the Victorville 2 prison educational department for all the help and the breaks that they gave me Mr. Gardner, Ms. Rufus, Mr. Brown, Ms. Stipe and the head man in charge Mr. Schultz.

Sincerely
D. M. Gaines

Prologue

It was Monday June 9th, 1990. It was 10:00am and the courtroom 16B on the 16th floor of the Cuyahoga County Justice Center was filled to capacity. Every seat was filled and people stood lining the walls waiting for the jury to read the verdict.

Harry Henderson was on trial for three counts of murder, and was facing the death penalty.

Some of the spectators felt that if Harry did kill those people, that it was justice, not murder. If your only daughter had been killed and your son was in the hospital fighting for his life, what would you do to the people that were responsible?

Three years earlier, Terresa, was sixteen and a sophomore in high school. Her brother Ricky was eighteen and out of school. Their family had been living in the Longwood Housing projects since she was three and he was five.

They were the children of two hard working parents. Her father Harry, worked at a steel plant and her mother worked as a school nurse.

Their mother and father tried hard to provide a good life for them. Though they stayed in the projects, their parents made sure that they had everything that they needed.

They had goals of buying their own house one day and moving their family out of the lower class housing projects. Until then, their parents had to hope that they would not get caught up or involved in all of the negative activities that went on in the projects.

To do that, they urged Ricky to join the boxing team at the P. O. C recreation center. Terresa was a cheerleader in school and took a drama class at the recreation center after school.

Things seemed to be going good until Terresa turned sixteen and Ricky turned eighteen. By then it was 1987 and the drug trade had become real prominent in their neighborhood. People that had never engaged in any type of crimes in their life, became lured into the drug game because of the lucrative profits that it made.

The money started to change the once strict and normal people's values and principals. Parents became more lenient and kids started staying out later on school nights.

Terresa's parents seen the dramatic change that was going on in their neighborhood. They moved up their plans to purchase a house, to the end of the upcoming year. They refused to give in to the lowering of the family values that was going on throughout the urban communities. They had goals set for their children and wanted to make sure that they achieved them.

Little did they know, the drug culture had already taken effect on their kids. Even though they gave their kids all that they could, it still wasn't enough to keep up with the quickly changing urban culture.

The Calvin Klein and Gloria Vanderbilt jeans had been ushered out by Levi, Guess and Polo jeans. Pony and Puma tennis shoes were pushed out by the arrival of Air Max and Air Jordans, which cost almost one hundred dollars. Soon the things that their parents bought for them to wear were outdated.

Terresa and Ricky both started feeling the effects of the changes. It put a dent in their self esteem. Curiosity and wanting to fit in got the best of Terresa and her brother.

One day after boxing practice Ricky came out of the recreation center and seen Marcus, who used to be on the boxing team with him, wiping off a brand new Nissan Maxima with thirty day tags on it. Ricky approached him, "Damn Marcus, your father let you drive his new car?"

"Ricky, you tripping dude this ain't my father's car, it's mine."

"What, he bought it for you!"

"Hell no fool! I bought this car myself."

"How did you do that? You don't have a job."

"I might don't have a job, but I got a hustle and it's better than having a job."

"What type of hustle do you have that's better than a job?"

"This," Marcus told him, then pulled a vial out of his pocket that was filled with hard white little pebbles. "Fuck is that shit?" Ricky asked him.

"This crack dawg. This the shit that's going to make young black niggas rich. I make about five hundred a day slanging these stones."

"Five hundred a day, nigga you lying?"

"Nigga, you ain't got nothing to do, roll with me and see how I do."

They got into Marcus' car and he pulled off. Marcus drove over to Case Court and parked. Him and Ricky got out and sat on the hood off his car.

Ricky sat there and watched in amazement as Marcus made sale after sale. After two hours Marcus had sold out and needed to go home to reup.

When they got into his car Ricky asked him, "How much did you make?" Marcus counted the money out in front of him and it came up to four hundred and thirty dollars.

"Damn man! That's crazy, how can I be down?"

"This ain't no game Ricky. This ain't something that is done for fun. This shit is serious and has risks that come with it. You ain't no street nigga. Stick to boxing, which is something that you are good at, I don't want to be the one that fuck your life up."

"Nigga cut all that preaching and shit. I'm a grown ass man, I been boxing for years and that shit hasn't put any money in my pocket and I'm tired of depending on my family to support me. I just watched you and the shit ain't that hard. A kid can do that shit."

"You right! You are a grown man and can make your own decisions. You want in you got it, but hold your own weight. You get robbed, you handle it. You get knocked by the man, you take your own weight. Tomorrow I'm going to throw you a package. I'm going to take you to my spot and show you how to cut and package shit up. Teach you the price ranges and how to make people think that they are getting more than they really are getting."

The next day Marcus picked up Ricky and took him to his stash spot. He taught him how to cook up dope, how to cut it up into different sizes and how much each size was worth. He handed Ricky a small twenty two automatic gun. Ricky nervously took the gun and looked at it, "What do I need this for?"

"I told you that shit ain't sweet. It's niggas out here that are fucked up and don't got shit. They looking for a quick and easy lick." Ricky started having second thoughts. He hadn't seen that part of the game when he watched Marcus make all of that money. He thought about it for a minute and figured that Marcus was just trying to keep him on point, so he put the gun in his pocket and they left out of the stash house.

Marcus drove him over to Outhwaite, which was one street over from Case Court and had him set up shop. Ricky began his career as a dope boy.

π

The day started out slow for Ricky. He did not know how to at-
tract customers. He knew nothing about promoting drugs.

Two hours had went by without him making a single sale. Marcus
pulled up to check on him. He parked the car and got out. A older guy
climbed out the passenger's side of the car. Ricky looked at him and
wondered what he could be doing with Marcus, seeing as how he
looked dirty and not kept.

Marcus walked up to Ricky, "So how has business been?"

"Shit, I haven't made a sale."

"I figured that, that's why I brought Pete. Pete is going to be your
runner."

"What the hell is a runner?"

"He is going to bring you business. It's his job to let everybody
know that you got that work. Off of every five stones that he helps
you get rid of you throw him one, it's that simple." Marcus called for
Pete to come over and he walked over to Marcus and Ricky.

"Pete this is my boy Ricky. You hold him down and he is going
to take care of you. I'm going to come back through and check on
you two in a couple of hours to see where you are at, is that cool?"
Ricky and Pete both nodded their heads. Marcus walked back to his
car, got in and pulled off.

Pete went straight to work. All of the smokers knew Pete and that
he only smoked Grade A dope. Business quickly picked up and by
the time Marcus came back to check on them, they had sold out.

"What's up playboy?" Marcus asked Ricky.

"Shit, I need some more stuff?" Ricky handed Marcus the money
that he had made. Marcus counted it, then gave Ricky his cut. He
went to his car and got another package and handed it to Ricky.

"You doing your thing man. Keep it up and you will be riding like me in no time." Ricky just smiled. He felt that he had finally found something that he could do to take care of his self. He stayed on the block until midnight.

Marcus had to bring him two more packages while he was out there. Ricky went home with six hundred dollars in his pocket. He felt that it was time to put up the boxing gloves, and concentrate on his new hustle.

Terresa was good friends with Judy, Micky and Coo Coo. They were all on the cheerleading team together.

Teressa started noticing how the three girls had all of a sudden started coming to school in the latest fashions and carrying two hundred dollar Louis Vuitton purses on their shoulders.

After cheerleading practice they would head outside to be picked up by men driving Acura Legends and Volvos, while she caught the bus to her drama class.

One day they were getting dressed after cheerleading practice, when Teresa asked Judy, "Who are those guys that be coming to pick you all up from school?"

"Girl them niggas are from Detroit. They are up here getting money. You should come with us today. They got a cute friend named Detroit Tone that just came up here. I know he will dig you."

"You know that I have my drama class."

"Girl, aren't you tired of that boring shit? These niggas got paper and don't mind spending it. Just miss one day and come with us." Teresa thought about it for a minute. Her drama class was boring, plus she was curious to see what the girls were involved in that they had guys willing to buy them two hundred dollar purses.

"Okay, I guess I can miss one day."

"That's what's up." Micky told her.

After school they all stood across the street from the school. They only stood waiting for a couple of minutes, before two cars pulled over in front of them. Judy and Micky climbed into the first car. Terresa got into the second car with Coo Coo. She climbed into the backseat and sat next to a guy that she could not take her eyes off of. The guy had skin the color of honey. If it wasn't for his chipped tooth, Terresa thought that he could have been a model. What got her most was his eyes which appeared to be gray.

Coo Coo turned around in her seat, "Tone that's my girl Ressa." Tone looked at Terresa. He was hyped, liking what he saw. To him Terresa was bad. She was very pretty and had long curly hair. Her titties sat up and from the way her hips were poking out while she was sitting down he could tell that she had a fat ass.

"How are you doing Ressa?" Tone asked her. Terresa blushed, put her head down then said, "I'm fine."

"You don't have no boyfriend do you?"

"No why?"

"Because I want to be your boyfriend."

"How old are you?"

"I'm nineteen, is that too old for you?"

"No, but I do not even know you like that."

"You never start out knowing anyone like that. You spend time with a person to get to know them. You find out if you are compatible. If you have the same likes and dislikes. It's a process, one that I am willing to go through with you. All I ask is that you give me a fair chance and we can see where it goes from there. Is that too much to ask?"

Terresa had never had game kicked to her like that. To her he seemed sophisticated and that excited her. "No, that ain't too much to ask." she told him.

They pulled to a stop behind the first car, which had stopped in front of a Best Steak and Gyro restaurant. They got out of the car and followed the other group inside. They got two tables, put them together and sat down. Judy started introducing Terresa to all of the guys, "Ressa this, is my boo Rocko, that is Micky's man Frank. You should of already met Tone and Slim since you just got through riding with them." Terresa looked all of the guys over. Rocko looked like a bodybuilder. He had muscles poking out from everywhere. Frank was cute with a baby face, he had two gold nugget fronts, and Slim was just as his name suggested, tall and slim.

Terresa noticed that they were all wearing Troop jackets and Lotto tennis shoes. People in Cleveland were not wearing those type of things, which made them stand out.

They ordered their food, with Tone ordering Terresa a steak and cheese sandwich and a soda. They sat around and talked while they ate. After they got finished eating they got back into the cars and headed down to Longwood.

They pulled into a parking lot on 33rd and filed out of the cars. They entered a apartment building and headed up to the third floor. Rocko knocked on the door and a slim, older lady wearing clothes that were hanging off of her body opened the door. A broad smile came across her face when she saw Rocko and his crew. They had been gone all morning and she hadn't had anything to smoke. She was glad that they were back.

"Rita what's up?" Rocko asked her as he entered the house with everybody following behind them. Rocko and his crew had been staying at Rita's house for over a month. They had turned her house into their trap house, using it to hustle out of. All they had to do was to make sure that Rita had something to smoke and give her a couple of dollars to buy food. It was worth it to them because they were making a killing out of her house.

Their only problem was that they needed to get a house where they could lay their heads. They knew that laying their heads in a house that they were selling dope out of was dangerous. Rocko had been procrastinating. He knew that he should have been gotten a girl to rent an apartment for them. He really did not like spending money, that's why he held off on getting a place. He was the leader, so even if the rest of his crew did not agree with his decision they rode with it.

The girls took a seat on the sofas and chairs in the living room. Rocko grabbed the remote and turned on the entertainment system. He gave Rita a couple stones and she left out of the house to go downstairs to smoke with her friend Pam.

Judy asked, "Is we going to party or what?" Rocko pulled a clear baggie out of his pocket and tossed it to Judy. Judy poured the substance out of the baggie onto the end table. She took her school I.D. out of her purse and split the substance up into several lines. She then pulled out her compact, opened it up and pulled out a small straw.

Terresa could not believe her eyes. She did not know what was going on. She had never actually seen drugs before in her life, let alone watch someone do them. She watched as Judy snorted a whole line of the substance while the other two girls eagerly awaited their turns.

"Shit!" Judy said as she caught a rush. She coughed and tilted her head back to catch the drain that the cocaine was giving her.

"That shit must be good," Micky said as she moved over to get her a line. Slim fired up a joint that was laced with cocaine. It was called a primo. The whole Detroit crew smoked primos.

The smoke from the primo started making Terresa feel sick. She needed some fresh air.

"You want to hit a line of this?" Coo Coo asked Terresa.

"I need some air, I'm starting to get sick."

"You just ain't use to it yet. You got virgin lungs." Judy told her.

"Come on baby girl, let's go outside." Tone told her. She got up off of the couch and her and Tone went outside. There was a race-track across the street that belonged to Cuyahoga Community College.

They went over to it and started circling the track as they talked.

Tone asked her about everything from her family to her goals. She asked Tone what his purpose for being in Cleveland was and his reply was, "To ensure a better living for my people back home."

"You are going to do that by selling drugs?"

"Baby girl, sometimes in life you have to do bad in order to do good." Terresa did not understand what he meant, but she felt attracted to him like a magnet to steel. They talked for about forty minutes by then it had started to get dark and chilly. They decided to head back into the house.

When they entered the house it was an orgy taking place. Rocko was standing in front of Judy, who was sitting on the couch. He had his pants and underwear down around his ankles, while Judy sucked him off. Frank had Micky doggy style on the couch as he stood up fucking her from behind and Slim was laid out flat on his back on the floor as Coo Coo rode his dick.

The whole scene shocked Terresa. She covered her mouth and tried to back out of the door. Tone blocked her path. He told her, "Come on, let's go into the back."

She put her hand over her eyes as he led her to a back bedroom. They got in there and he closed the door. Terresa stood by the door scared. Tone sensed it and told her, "Relax, I'm not going to bite you. I guess you did not know that your girls got down like that."

"I don't see how they can just have sex out in the open like that."

"They are just being free. Let me ask you a question are you a virgin?" Terresa knew that it was too early for him to be asking her something like that, yet for some reason she felt compelled to tell him.

"I have had sex twice."

"Why only twice, what you did not like it?"

"I did not get anything from it. I felt nothing, so I guess I miss nothing."

"Whoever they were, they must did not know what they were doing. They didn't take their time with you and give you the business."

"Both times, were with the same guy, but it seemed that all of you guys do the same thing, you brag about what you can do but never live up to it."

"Baby girl I can give you all the pleasure that you ever could ask for and not ask for anything back. All you have to do is tell me that you trust me and that it is okay and I will make today the best day that you have ever experienced."

For some strange reason she felt safe with Tone. She felt as if she had known him for years.

It took Lonie two years to talk her into having sex, yet there it was she had just met Tone only hours earlier and had the urge to have sex with him.

"You say, I don't have to do anything?"

"Just lay there and accept the pleasure that I give you."

"I got to see this." Terresa said.

Tone approached her and started unbuttoning her jeans. After he finished, he pulled them and her panties down to her a ankles. Terresa had to sit on the bed so that he could undo her shoes. Once they were off, he pulled her pants and panties off. For a minute he just looked at her. The curves of her hips the curly hair of her thick bush. Tone knew that he was going to have a field day with her. His specialty was turning young girls out. He knew that she had never came either.

He pushed her down on the bed and spread her legs. He bent them back exposing her young, juicy looking pussy lips. His mouth started watering just looking at her pussy. He took his forefinger and put it to her entrance. He moved it around the inside of her pussy lips, getting it wet. He took his index, finger and put it to the entrance also. He slid both fingers into her pussy and started moving them around in different motions. Terresa felt herself responding. She felt her pussy getting wet. Tone took his thumb and placed it on her clit. He started rubbing it in a circular motion, while he fucked her with his two fingers. Terresa's clit came alive. It filled up with blood, which caused it to stick out. She let out a soft moan.

She had never felt pleasure come from down there. Her whole body started to feel good. Tone seen her back arch and knew that he had her. He put his head between her legs, and blew on her clit. A shiver went through Terresa's body. Tone put his mouth on her pussy. He sucked her clit into his mouth and began to gently nibble on it. Terresa did not know what was going on when her body started to shudder. An euphoria came over her. She felt like she was having an outer body experience when she started cumming. The pleasure was so intense that she closed her eyes and put both of her hands on Tone's head and tried to push him off of her. Tone kept a grip on her and kept eagerly sucking her pussy. Within minutes Terresa was coming again. That time she felt as though she was going to faint. After she came for the second time her body went completely limp.

Tone wiped her cum off of his mouth and stood up. Terresa just looked at him in amazement. She did not even try to reach for her clothes or try to cover up. Her body was too drained to do anything. Tone looked down at her and asked, "Do you believe me now?" Terresa waited for her breath to even out then told him, "Yeah,"

Tone smiled and told her, "When I tell you something, believe in me like you believe in God, because it's going to manifest."

She got dressed and they went out to the living room with everyone else. The orgy was over and everybody was back dressed.

"Damn girl, you are glowing. He must of dicked you down good." Judy said to Terresa, who only smiled nervously. Terresa was officially part of their click. From that day on there would be no more drama classes for Terresa.

3

Ricky became a full fledge hustler. He gave up boxing altogether. When he went to the rec center to clear out his locker, his coach approached him, "Where have you been and why are you clearing out your locker?"

"I'm done boxing Smitty. I been doing this shit for years and I have gained nothing from it. I'm a grown man still living with my parents and letting them take care of me. I ain't got time to keep waiting for a break. I got to make my own way."

"So what, you got a job or something?"

"No, I don't have a job, but I got a way to take care of myself."

"Ricky, tell me you ain't out in them streets selling drugs? You are too smart for that. You can turn pro and we could get you some fights. You may start out making peanuts but after you have proven yourself, you can get better pay days."

"It's too late for all of that. Marcus showed me a better way."

"Don't be no fool Ricky. Marcus is not a good thinker that is why he wasn't a good boxer. You are a good thinker and it wouldn't be wise to follow Marcus, because he is going to end up either in jail or dead."

"I will take my chances." Ricky told him as he took the last of his things out of his locker and slammed it shut.

He walked off, leaving Smitty standing there shaking his head.

Ricky started hanging out with Marcus more. They would go to clubs together. Marcus like having Ricky kick it with him, because he knew that he was good with his hands. He knew that if he ran into any trouble that Ricky would go.

He urged Ricky to spend some of the money that he was making on getting himself some new attire. Ricky went shopping and started buying some of the latest fashions. He purchased a starter coat, a pair of Air Jordans and various pairs of fashion jeans. He even bought himself a big dookie rope.

He started hustling longer hours and making more money. He was hustling so good that Marcus started to fall back and put more drugs into his hands.

Ricky was loving it. He had a shoebox stashed in his closet that was filled to the top with money. He was thinking about buying himself a car, but he didn't want to have his father on his back. His father had been working a lot of overtime, so they hadn't been seeing much of each other. His mother however had been seeing him. She seen the changes in him. She seen him wearing things that she knew she nor her husband had bought for him. She also took notice of the new attitude that he seemed to have.

One night she heard him come in the house late at night. She got up out of her bed and went to his room. She opened his bedroom door, "Ricky," she said.

Ricky was in the act of stashing his box of money and his mother had startled him. He jumped almost to the ceiling, "What the hell!"

"Boy! What are you doing?" she asked him.

"I ain't doing nothing ma. You just startled me sneaking up on me like that."

"You wouldn't be startled if you weren't doing something that you ain't supposed to be doing."

"Ma, you are tripping. I'm not doing anything but getting ready for bed."

"Ricky, I ain't stupid. You are doing something, you are walking around here wearing those high priced clothes and shoes. You are doing something and I advise you to stop it before your father finds out. He is breaking his back to make sure that you and your sister have a good life, and if he found out you were out in them streets doing wrong he would kill you." Ricky got mad, "You call living in the projects having a good life? You call me being grown still living at home with you and him having a good life?"

"Boy, have you lost your damn mind! You got a roof over your head, clothes on your back and you never go hungry. That is more than what a lot of people have."

"Well, that ain't enough for me. I want to be my own man and take care of myself."

"You find yourself a job and you can do that."

"The only skill I got is boxing and that ain't bringing in no money."

"Well, I'm not going to just sit back and watch you destroy your life and break me and your father's heart. If you don't have your shit together by next week, I'm going to inform your father that he needs to have a talk with you."

"Ma, I'm grown, can't nobody tell me what to do."

"As long as you live in this house, you can be told what to do."

"Maybe I need to find somewhere else to live then."

"You got a week," his mother told him, then left out of his room, closing the door behind her.

Ricky flopped down onto his bed. He folded his hands behind his head and stared at the ceiling as he contemplated the inevitable. He knew that he would soon be clashing with his father, something that he was going to hate having to do.

π

His mother went into her room, sat on her bed and started crying. She felt that she was losing her baby to the streets. She knew that she had to stop it. She knew if she told her husband that he was out in the streets doing wrong that he would blow his top, and that it would put a wedge between her and her only son.

Being a parent she understood that you had to make hard decisions sometimes. She decided that she was going to tell his father before things got out of hand.

π

The next day Ricky was riding with Marcus on his way up to the strip. Marcus sensed that he was in a foul mood. He decided to inquire to see what was up.

"What's wrong playboy? I can tell that you have something on your mind."

"My moms tripped on me last night. She knows that I'm out here in these streets. She threatened to tell my old man."

"So, what are you going to do?"

"I might have to start looking for me a place to stay." Marcus' mind immediately started turning. He thought of his girl's sister Felicia. She had her own place and did not have a man. He thought that Ricky and her might be a perfect fit.

"I think I can help you out playboy." he told Ricky as he headed towards Felicia's house.

π

Terresa had been hanging out with the girls for the past two weeks. She did not even attend her drama class anymore or even go to get her things.

One day her and the girls were at the trap house while all the men were out handling some business. Rocko had left Judy a pack of powder. She broke it out and her and the other girls started getting high. Terresa was the only one that wasn't getting high, and they all started riding her about it.

"You got to stop being all stuck up." Judy said to her.

"Girl what are you talking about?"

"You ain't participating." Micky jumped in saying.

"I don't do drugs!"

"That's just it. What you think that you are too good or some-thing?"

"Drugs are addictive and messes up peoples."

"And, who told you that?"

"Everybody knows that."

"That's bullshit. Drugs don't mess up people lives. People mess up their own lives, besides coke ain't like heroin or crack. It is a recreational drug that loosens you up and makes you feel good. Everyone gets high but you. Even Tone gets high. You are going to have to get with the program or get gone." Judy told her.

Judy had never talked to her like that before, and to her surprise all of the girls were acting funny towards her and she did not understand why.

"For your information, Tone don't like no square broads, so once he finds a girl that likes to party with him you are going to be out of the picture." Micky told her.

Terresa started wondering if what they were saying was true. She hoped not because she had fell for Tone. He sexed her everyday for a week straight, then he had to make a run back home for a couple of days. While he was gone her body craved for him like a drug.

He had turned her sexually. He did everything from sucking her toes to licking her ass. He taught her how to suck dick and they did the sixty nine. She even started initiating the sex between them and became very vocal. Her shyness was completely gone.

Also he had been spending lots of money on her. He had taken her shopping and bought her a gold locket. He bought her different color Fila tennis shoes, and two Guess outfits. There was no way in the world that she wanted to lose him. She was starting to feel that the girls were going to turn on her if she did not engage in getting high with them. She had been around them for weeks and had not seen any negative signs. So she thought that it couldn't be that bad.

"Show me how to do it." she said to Judy. All the girl's faces lit up, "Here, just take this and start at the beginning of that line then to the other end. When you get through with that, then you switch the straw to the other nostril and snort the other line." Teressa took the straw from her and went over to the table. She knelt down over the table and put the straw to her nose.

"Use a finger from your other hand to hold your other nostril closed." Coo Coo told her. Terresa held her left nostril closed while she snorted the first line through her right nostril. She was only halfway through the line, when she went into a fit of coughing and choking. Judy had to pat her on her back.

"Beat your chest girl." She told Terresa. Terresa made a fist and hit herself in the chest trying to clear her airways.

"It must of went down the wrong passage." Judy told her after Terresa got her composure, they encouraged her to finish and she did. She snorted both lines of coke. She sat on the couch and leaned her head back, because her head felt heavy. She felt light as if she would just float away at anytime. She actually felt good. The feeling was almost as good as the one that she felt when Tone would make her cum.

They all finished the rest of the pack and when the men came in they were all over them. Terresa went at Tone hard. She was horny as hell. Tone had never seen her like that before he knew that she had to be on something.

"Is you high?" he asked her. She just giggled and went for his belt buckle.

"I want you to fuck me Tone."

"Let's go into the room." he told her.

"We can do it right here."

"If that's what you want baby girl." Tone stripped her right there in the living room and started fucking her in front of everybody. He had her doggy style on the floor. Terresa was oblivious, to anyone else being in the room with them. She was breathing and sweating hard.

"Tone, oh baby it feels sooo ... good!" Their show was so good that everyone else just sat around and watched them. Tone had to perform for the audience. He brought all the freak out of Terresa.

"You love this dick don't you?"

"Shit! Yes!"

"Do I fuck you right?"

"'Hell yeah!"

"You like how my dick taste?"

"Uh huh!"

"Put it in your mouth then." Tone stood up and Terresa turned around and raised up on her knees. She reached out and grabbed Tone's dick. First she jacked it off with her hand then she took her hand and started massaging his balls as she took him into her mouth. She sucked his dick like a porno star would do to her partner while making a movie.

The other fellas couldn't stand it anymore. For them the show was over. They got with their girls and started doing their own thing. There were four couples all in the living room naked doing their thing.

Terresa did something that she had never done before, she let Tone cum in her mouth and she swallowed it all. His dick had shriveled up, but she still kept sucking on it trying to bring it back to life.

Tone thought to himself, "Coke turns her into a straight freak, I wonder what a primo would do to her." Terresa did not know that from that day forth her life would become a living hell.

4

Marcus took Ricky over to Felicia's house. They pulled into her driveway and Marcus cut the car off. He told Ricky, "Come on." They both got out of the car and Ricky followed him up to the door. Marcus rang the doorbell and a high yellow woman with hazel eyes opened the door.

Ricky could not take his eyes off of her as she walked up to Marcus and gave him a hug, "Hey bro." she said as she squeezed him tightly. To Ricky that did not look like the type of hug that you gave your brother.

"I just stopped by to introduce you to my boy Ricky."

Marcus told her as he broke their embrace. Felicia looked at him like he was crazy. She rolled her eyes and told him. I don't need you to play matchmaker for me."

"Is you going to invite us in or what?"

"Come on in, but I don't need no hook up." she said to him with an attitude. They followed her into the living room. Felicia had on a cream colored pair of slacks that were almost see through. Ricky swore that he could see her ass cheeks through the fabric. The way that her ass jiggled as she walked, he swore to himself that she couldn't have any panties on.

She told them that they could have a seat. They both sat down on the sofa and she asked them, "Would you both like something to drink?"

"Yeah, get me a beer." Marcus told her.

"And what about you?" she asked Ricky.

"Thanks, but I'm good."

"If you say so," she said then turned and headed into the kitchen.

Marcus got up and followed her into the kitchen. Felicia pulled a bottle of beer out of the refrigerator and walked over to the counter to open it. Marcus walked up behind her and wrapped his arms around her. He pulled her to him and whispered into her ear, "I've missed this pussy."

"I don't know what type of games you are playing but I ain't for them. Fuck you mean you want me to meet your boy?"

"Calm down Felicia. Ricky is my worker and he brings in good money. He's going through a little situation at home and might need a place to stay. I figured I would hook him up with you. When I'm not around, he can look after you."

"So what, I'm supposed to fuck both of you?"

"I don't care what you do with him, just give him a place to stay and keep him happy. We both know that pussy belongs to me."

"See you got the game fucked up! You a grimy nigga, you don't care about nobody but yourself."

"I do care about other people. I just care about getting money more."

"So, do he know that we are fucking?"

"No, all he knows is that you are my girl's sister and we can keep it like that."

"So, you want me to kick it with him, but you want to be able to fuck me behind his back?"

"Why not, while he's out there getting that money, I could be tending to that pussy."

"You a shiesty nigga."

"Look who's talking, you're not exactly a angel either. Karen is your sister isn't she?"

"Whatever nigga!" Felicia said as she walked back out into the living room. She thought to herself, "If Marcus wants to play games, then we both can play games."

She was tired of him treating her like a piece of meat and using her house as a stash spot. He treated her sister Karen like a queen. Had her living out in Cleveland Heights, paid the car note on her brand new car and took her to all of the big events. She was jealous of him and her sister's relationship.

She decided that she was going to see what Ricky really was about. She had already taken in the fact that he looked good.

She sat on the sofa next to him and started the game, "So Ricky do you have a girlfriend?"

"No, I don't have a girlfriend."

"Is you gay or something?"

"Fuck no! You tripping!"

"Why don't you have a girlfriend then? You in the game and you are fine as hell." Marcus just sat back he knew that Felicia was on some bullshit, but he didn't care because he was getting tired of her ass anyway.

"I'm on a paper chase." Ricky told her.

"If you are on a paper chase now, then you are going to forever be on a paper chase. You hustlers are not satisfied with any amount of money that you get. You are going to end up being a rich, sore dick nigga. You got to live life while you're getting money. You don't put life on hold while you getting money."

"Fuck is you some type of psychic or psychiatrist?"

"Nope, I'm just a woman that has been real observant most of her life. Marcus, told me that you may need a place to stay. If you find that to be true, then maybe we could make some type of arrangement. I do have a extra room since you are on a paper chase. You just let me know."

"It's time to roll playboy, there is money to be made." Marcus told him.

"I'm ready when you are." They got up and headed out to the car. Marcus walked out last and as Felicia was closing the door he winked at her.

Marcus dropped Ricky off on the strip, where he hustled until two in the morning.

π

Ricky headed home tired and hungry. When he got to the house he seen that the living room light was on and wondered what that was about. He entered the house and walked into the living room, where he found his father sitting on the couch with a menacing look on his face. Ricky knew instantly that his mother must of said something.

His father stood up when he entered the living room. His father was 48 years old, but was still in good condition. Working in a steel mill for almost twenty years kept him fit. He stood at six three and weighed two hundred and seventy pounds. He had Popeye like forearms and hands big enough to crush the life out of anyone.

As he walked towards Ricky, he took steps back, "You out there in them streets boy. You think you can just disrespect your mother?" His father asked him as he started to take his belt off.

"Pops, I'm a grown man. You are not about to hit me with no belt."

"You know what, you are right. You are grown, I ain't going to use no belt, you good with your hands right?"

His father dropped the belt and balled his hands up into fist.

"Let's see what you got." his father told him as he got into his fighting stance and started moving in on Ricky. Ricky backed up until there was nowhere else to go. His back was pinned against the wall.

"Pops you are tripping."

"No, I ain't tripping, you the one tripping. Your mother told me what's been going on. I went up to the gym today. Smitty told me how you running around with that no good boy Marcus selling that poison, killing your own people and yourself. I would rather kill you myself before I sit up and let somebody else kill you. I done did all I could for you. I been working myself into a early grave trying to provide for you and you disrespect me like this?"

"I'm a grown man Pops, I don't need you taking care of me. I can take care of myself."

"Let's see if that's true, his father told him then hit him with a right hook to his ribs. He followed up with a straight left to Ricky's chest. Ricky grabbed his chest as if he was having a heart attack. He fell to the floor and curled up into a fetal position.

"You can take care of yourself right?" his father said to him as he advanced on him.

"Stop it Harry! That's enough! You are going to kill him."

"Marlene it's better that I kill him then to let someone out in them streets kill him." Ricky's mother ran over and fell on top of Ricky to prevent his father from being able to inflict more pain on him.

"Marlene you can save him from me, but you can't save him from them streets. I love you Ricky, I love you to death son, but if you are going to continue to sale that poison then I want you out of this house by the time that I get in from work tomorrow." His father turned and walked upstairs to his bedroom.

Ricky's mother helped him up and she supported him as he limped over to the couch. He fell onto the couch and winced in pain. He had never had a rib broken before, but from the type of pain that he was feeling he knew that something had to be wrong with his ribs.

"Your father loves you baby, we both love you. We just want you to do what's right. Your father has struggled all of his life to make sure that you had a better life than him and you are about to throw it all away out in them streets. I'm begging you Ricky, leave those drugs alone. Get yourself a job."

With that she went upstairs with her husband. She entered their bedroom and found Harry sitting on the bed crying. Tears ran down both of his cheeks. She went over to him, sat down next to him and put her arm around him. They had been together for over 26 years and she had never seen her husband breakdown as he was doing then. He had his face in both of his hands.

"Marlene how can we save him? How can we help him if he won't let us?"

"We have to pray Harry. We have to pray and hope that God answers our prayers. If he is here when we come in from work tomorrow, then we know that God has answered our prayers."

They did not have to wait until they got home from work the following day to know the answer. When they got up the next morning Ricky was already gone. His mother went to his room and found that all his dresser drawers were pulled out and were all empty. She went over to his closet and opened it. She found, nothing but empty hangers on the racks.

She started crying and yelling, "Harry he's gone, my baby is gone." Terresa heard her mother yelling and went to see what was going on. She went to her brother's room and seen her mother sitting on his bed crying. She looked at the empty drawers and the empty closet.

"Where is Ricky momma?"

"He is in them streets," her father said as he walked up behind her. He told his wife, "There is nothing we can do now. It's out of our hands."

On the inside he was hurting deeply. He was starting to feel like a failure. He just hoped that his son would come to his senses before he ended up dead or in jail.

5

Detroit Tone was never really a follower. He was always ambitious, and would just play his role until he got the opportunity to make a move.

He did not agree with Rocko's tactics and how he operated, that was why he was the last one to join them up in Cleveland.

It was Slim who convinced him to come telling him how sweet it was up in Cleveland. Tone figured that he would go up there and get to know his way around and that once he did he would break away from Rocko.

Tone did just that. He got familiar with Cleveland and the people in its drug culture. He started making connections and developing relationships.

He met a guy named Manky, that put him on with his sister Sherell. She agreed to rent him an apartment in her name and in exchange he would pay her a hundred dollars every month.

She rented, him a one bedroom apartment on 120th and Buckeye. Tone furnished the house with a bed, a couch, a television and a stove. The stove was not for cooking food, it was for cooking his dope.

Tone also paid Sherell to rent him a 1987 Maxima, so that he could get around on his own.

Rocko was upset when he found out that Tone was branching out on his own. He liked to keep people under him and dictating what they could and couldn't do. He felt that Tone had played him and he confronted him about it. Tone was down at Rita's house one day chilling with Slim and Frank.

Rocko came to the house and seen Tone. He frowned his face up and said, "What is this cross out artist doing up in here?"

"Fuck is you talking about?" Tone asked him.

"Nigga, you know what I'm talking about. You used a nigga to get on then you bailed."

"Rocko, you know that I never been the one to stay under someone else, I like to move on my own, it's still all love. Anything goes down I'm there with you. I'm just trying to do my thing that's all."

"Do your thing then nigga, I don't need you. If something jumps I can handle it myself." Rocko headed in the back, grabbed a package then left back out of the house.

Slim lit up a primo and they all started smoking it. Frank took long drags off of it and realized that he did hot get the same effects anymore. Primos no longer gave him the ultimate high.

"I'm tired of wasting dope." he told them as he pulled a pipe out of his pocket.

"Nigga, you about to hit that glass dick?" Tone asked him.

"What the fuck is the difference. Smoking rocks is smoking rocks. Putting them in weed and cigarettes only lessens the high. This gives you the full effect, just watch." Frank put a rock on the top of the stem and flicked his lighter. He put the stem to his mouth and the lighter to the end of the stem. The rock started to crackle as the fire hit it. Frank started pulling on the stem and a thick cloud of gray smoke started going through the stem giving him a straight contact.

Slim and Tone watched as he sucked, the thick cloud through the pipe. They seen what he meant about getting the full effect.

The effects of the crack hit Frank so hard that he had to sit the pipe and the lighter down and walk over to the window. He opened it and stuck his head out of it.

Slim and Tone just looked at the stem as it laid on the table still smoking.

"Fuck it let's see what that shit really do." Tone said to Slim then reached for the stem and the lighter. He put the stem to his mouth and the lighter to the stem. When the stem began filling up with smoke he started inhaling it. He took two strong pulls and started hearing bells. A ringing sound appeared in his ears as he felt the most intense high that he ever felt in his life. The high was so intense that it scared him. He threw the pipe onto the floor. Slim got up and went over and picked it up.

He was curious to see what it was about after seeing both of his partners tripping. He put the stem to his mouth and grabbed the lighter and put it to the end of the stem. He started pulling on the stem, but very little smoke came through it. He realized that he needed to put some more crack into it. He went into his pocket and pulled out a vial that contained crack. He took a rock out of the vial and put it to the stem. He lit it and started smoking it. He pulled so hard on the stem that he went into a fit of coughing. It was a powerful drug, he found out for sure.

Frank had came back from the window seeking another hit. As soon as Tone's high went down he was ready for another hit.

They sat in Rita's house for over two hours smoking crack. Had Rocko come back and seen how they were smoking up all the money he may have tried to kill them all.

π

Tone started smoking crack regularly and he introduced Terresa to it. He already had her smoking primos and sucking cocaine off of his dick. She would do anything to stay in good graces with Tone.

They were in the bed at Tone's apartment. Tone was stretched out on his back, while Terresa was in between his legs sucking his dick. Tone reached over and slid open the nightstand drawer. He pulled out a pipe, a lighter and a baggie with rocks in it. He put a rock in the pipe and started smoking it while Terresa was giving him head. He was experiencing an ultimate high. The high from the crack along with the pleasure of getting his dick sucked had him on cloud nine.

He came in Terresa's mouth and she swallowed it all. He wanted her to feel what he had felt. He refilled the pipe and handed it to her. He told her what to do with it.

"Put that end up to your mouth, and light the other end with the lighter. Wait for it to fill up with smoke before you start pulling on it. You got it?"

"Yeah, I got it baby."

They switched positions. Terresa laid back on a pillow with her legs open and started smoking on the pipe, while Tone was down in between her legs eating her pussy.

Once the high from the crack hit her, she was in ecstasy. She came multiple times back to back. She had never experienced the type of feeling that she was feeling then, in her life. She wished that she could feel like she was feeling at that moment for the rest of her life.

Her and Tone smoked crack and sexed each other for hours, then dozed off. When she woke up she seen that it was one in the morning. It was a school night and she knew that her parents would kill her if they realized that she was not at home in bed. She tried to shake Tone awake so that he could take her home, but he was in a coma.

Terresa started crying, hoping that her parents would not check her room in the morning and see that she wasn't in it. She laid there next to Tone and cried herself to sleep.

6

Ricky moved in with Felicia. He took her spare room. He went into overdrive with the hustling. Sometimes he would pull twenty four hour stints. He bought himself a 1984 Chevy Caprice Classic, and still had about four thousand dollars put up.

Felicia started to respect his grind. She thought that if he kept going at that pace that he would soon catch up with and past Marcus.

Marcus was loving having his cake and eating it too. Ricky was making him mass money and while he would be out in the streets hustling for him, Marcus would be either fucking Felicia or getting her to suck his dick.

One night when Ricky came in, Felicia was sitting up in the living room watching a movie. She was sitting on the couch wearing a see through teddy. Her yellow titties and big brown nipples could easily be seen through the sheer material. He went to walk past her, "What up Felicia?"

"Your funny acting ass, that's what's up."

"Girl, what are you talking about?"

"I'm talking about you staying here with me but ignoring me. It's only hi and bye with you."

"Okay, so what do you want me to do?"

"Sit down and watch a movie with me."

Ricky looked to the TV, "That ain't the type of movie that I watch."

"1 got a whole collection of movies, just tell me what you want to see." she said to him as she got up off of the couch and approached the entertainment set.

"You got Scarface?"

"Yeah, 1 got it some where." she told him as she bent over to look through her VCR tapes. When she bent over all Ricky saw was ass and pussy.

Felicia did not have any underwear on. Ricky's dick instantly got hard as he stared at her fat pussy lips and an ass that did not have one blemish on it. He had to control his self. He wanted to just go over there, pull his dick out and ram it up in her. Unconsciously, he put his hand on his dick and started squeezing it.

"Here it go right here." Felicia said as she looked back while still being bent over. She seen Ricky's dick trying to bulge through his jeans.

"I guess he ain't gay," she said to herself.

"Your dick hurt huh?"

"Felicia, what type of games are you playing?"

"I'm ain't playing no games, I'm just trying to get your ass to notice me some type of way. I'm a woman with needs. You a man living in my house and acting like I don't exist. How do you think that makes me feel. To have a fine man living in my house without making a move on me."

"Felicia, you are beautiful, I'm just trying to keep it respectful."

"Fuck being respectful! Fuck me! Make me feel good. Make me feel wanted." she told him as tears started to run down her face.

Ricky did not know that she was as emotionally disturbed as he had just found out. She was looking out for him by letting him stay there. The only thing that she gave him flack about was him not paying her any attention.

"I guess I could show her my appreciation," he said to himself.

"He walked up to her and kissed her on her tear stained cheek, then he kissed her in her mouth. She opened her mouth and let his tongue invade it. Ricky put his hands around her and grabbed her ass. He started squeezing her naked ass cheeks. He lifted her up by her ass and she wrapped her legs around his waist, and put her arms around his neck.

He carried her into the bedroom and put her down on his bed. She unwrapped herself from him and he begun to undress. Felicia laid there on the bed and watched as he undressed. She realized that she had never even seen him bare chested in all the time that he had been living with her.

When he took his shirt off, she could not believe how cut up he was. He did not have a six pack, he had an eight pack. His upper body was chiseled. It was as if he had been carved out of stone. When he pulled off his pants and underwear, Felicia's mouth dropped opened. She fell in love with his dick and couldn't wait to get it into her mouth.

She got up on her knees and crawled to the end of the bed. She reached out with her hand and grabbed his dick. It felt so powerful in her hand. She used her hand and pulled him to her. She took his dick into her mouth. She closed her eyes as she made love to it. She could not control herself. She was on his dick like a dog on a bone. She sucked it from the front and the sides. She sucked his balls and licked up under them. Ricky was in bliss. He reached down and rubbed his fingers through her hair as she made love to his dick.

Felicia sucked on him until her jaws got sore. She was surprised by his stamina. Most men would cum in less than two minutes from the head she gave, but Ricky did not even seem as if he had reached the point of no return. She backed up off of his dick and laid back on the bed. Ricky approached her. He took her legs and twisted them like a pretzel. He crossed them into the Indian style position and pushed them back to her chest.

He climbed, onto the bed and got on top of her. He put his dick to her pussy's entrance and pushed in. Her pussy opened up and eagerly accepted him.

"Ricky you're filling me up. God you're in my stomach!" she told him as he sank all the way into her. Her legs were in his chest as he started fucking her. He put his arms on the bed and started rocking back and forth inside of her. They rocked like a rocking chair. Felicia had never experienced that position before nor the pleasure that she got from it.

"Damn nigga! You the coldest!" Ricky picked up his rhythm rocking back and forth and the next thing that she knew she was cumming and cumming hard.

"Uh ... Uhh ... Dammit, right there Ricky, right there baby, it's cumming!" Ricky started pulling all the way out of her then slamming back in. He felt his nuts tighten up and knew that he was cumming. He kept hitting her with powerful strokes. By the time that he started cumming, Felicia was getting a second nut.

After Ricky's balls were drained, he rolled off of Felicia. She just laid there trying to catch her breath. She had made a decision that either Ricky was moving into her room or she was moving into his. She also said to herself, "It's over with for Marcus little dick ass."

Felicia spent the night in Ricky's room. The next morning when they awoke, Felicia started planting a seed in his head.

"Ricky, you know that it is time for you to go out on your own. All that money that you are putting into Marcus' pocket could be going into your own."

"Marcus is good people. He put me on and I'm not going to turn on him."

"Marcus is not as good as you think he is and you do not owe him anything. It is about progressing in life not being stagnated. Don't be no follower all of your life. Be your own man."

"Felicia, where is all that coming from?"

"From me, I like you and I know that Marcus ain't shit. He will cross you out the first chance he gets."

"And how do you know all that?"

"Let's just say that I know."

"You make me think that it's more than some brother and sister shit going on between you two."

"Think what you want to think, but I'm telling you that he is no good. For some reason I'm starting to care about you and I just know that you can do better on your own." Ricky thought to his self that what she was saying made sense. Maybe it was time for him to branch out on his own. He started wondering how Marcus would feel if he made that move.

He grabbed his stash and his car keys, then told Felicia, "I hear you, I got to go up to the block. I will see you later."

When Ricky left the house, Felicia began moving his things up to her room. Ricky was up on the block, when a maroon Maxima pulled up and parked in front of him. Two guys got out of the Maxima. One of them looked as if he had just came home from prison. He was so big. The other guy was tall and skinny.

Ricky had never seen anyone of them before.

They walked towards Ricky and he stuck his hand inside of his jacket pocket. Rocko and Slim noticed the move.

"Be easy dawg, we just came to holla at you about some business." Rocko told him.

"We don't know each other to be having any type of business dealings."

"That is what I am trying to establish with you right now. I know that you are a hustler."

"And how do you know that?"

"I have been seeing you out here hustling everyday."

"What, you watching me like the police?"

"You are a funny dude. I'm going to let that one slide. Look, my name is Rocko and that's Slim. We are from the D and I'm up here getting paper. I'm tired of pushing pebbles and is ready to sell weight. I'm looking for people that are in need of a plug. People that are trying to get a endless supply of good dope. I'm willing to beat out the prices that you are already paying for your work."

" I'm supposed to just up and trust you like that?"

"You are a hard one, but I like your style so here is what I'm willing to do. I will give you a pack on consignment. You do it up and slang it and if you are satisfied with the outcome then we can go from there." Ricky thought about it and realized that he had nothing to lose, but could possibly gain a lot.

"How much are you willing to give me and how long will I have to get rid of it?"

"Say, I give you an eighth and give you four days, to get rid of it. You bring me thirty two hundred back." Ricky did the math in his head. He knew that off of four and a half ounces he could at least make seven thousand dollars selling stones. That would be double what he be making fucking with Marcus.

"So, when are you going to be able to do that?"

"All you have to do is give the word and I will pop my trunk right now."

"Let's do it then." They walked over to Rocko's car and he went into the trunk and pulled out a eighth of a kilo of cocaine and handed it to Ricky.

Rocko and Slim went to get back into the car and Ricky called after them, "Hey man, you don't even know my name."

"I know your name Ricky. I know a lot about you." Rocko told him then got into his car and pulled off. Ricky stood there in the street holding the dope in his hand. He was dumbfounded as to how Rocko had knew his name and implied that he knew more than just that.

He decided that he would finish the pack that he had gotten from Marcus then he would let him know that he was going solo.

7

Marcus was at Felicia's house. He was trying to get on but Felicia wasn't haying it. She kept brushing off his advances.

"Don't tell me that you are falling for the help. The 'lil nigga can't be fucking you as good as I do."

"If you only knew," I wonder how you would feel if I cut his ass off. Would you still fuck with him if he was broke?"

"Marcus, Ricky won't be going broke no time soon. He been stacking his money."

"If he got so much money put up why is he still working for me?"

"He's trying to be loyal to you, something that you know nothing about."

"I can't believe your trick ass really fell for that lame."

"Looks can be deceiving. You might be buying from him pretty soon."

"Bitch! You been smoking dope?"

"Nope, I just know what's real. Ricky is a real nigga with a real … big dick!" she said laughing. Marcus got angry and cocked his hand back.

"Nigga, you hit me you are going to jail!" Marcus knew that she was serious, but he wasn't going to let her get out on him that easily.

"Bitch, give me all of my shit." he told her as he went around the house grabbing all of the things that he had bought for her.

"Nigga take all of that shit and get your petty ass out of my house."

They both heard the front door open and turned to it. Ricky came walking into the house. He seen Marcus with a lamp up under his arm and wondered, what was going on.

"What's up?" he asked Marcus.

"I just dropped by to see if you was done with the pack and to get this lamp that I had let her use." Ricky looked at him like he was crazy. He knew that it had to be more to it than he was letting on to, but he wasn't going to sweat it.

"Yeah, I'm done with the pack. I was just about to call you." He reached in his pocket and pulled out a knot of money. He handed it to Marcus.

"I already took my cut out."

"That's cool, I'm going to have to bring you another pack in the morning."

"I'm good on that."

"What do you mean you're good?"

"I'm 'bout to start doing my own thing. I appreciate what you done for me, but it's time for me to be my own man."

"Man, you done let this conniving, back stabbing bitch turn you against me?"

"Marcus, I don't know what's up with you two. I do know that it's more than some brother and sister shit. Ain't neither one of you fooling me. It's obvious that the two of you are fucking. If you are, it's none of my business. It does show me that you was trying to play me though. She ain't got shit to do with my decision."

"Yeah, I be fucking the bitch, so what."

"You ain't shit!" Felicia yelled at Marcus then ran to her room.

"That bitch is crazy. I put you on with her because I don't care nothing about the bitch. You can have her, but that block that you are hustling on belongs to me."

"I built that strip up. I put in the work to make it what it is and I ain't giving it up."

"We will see about that!" Marcus told him as he headed for the door.

"I don't take threats too lightly!" Ricky called out after him.

"1 don't give them lightly either!" Marcus told him as he left out of the house.

Ricky went to his room and found that all of his things were gone.

"Fuck is my shit at?" he said to himself.

He left out of the room and headed towards Felicia's.

"Felicia! Felicia!" he called out. She appeared in her doorway. She had tears running down her face, "What?"

"Where the hell are my things?"

"I moved them into my room."

"Well you might as well move them back into mine. You're crazy if you think that I'm going to fuck with you like that, scandalous as you are."

"Hold the fuck up! I ain't scandalous nigga. We just started fucking last night. I'm the one that tried to tell you that he wasn't shit."

"You only told me that because you must be jealous that he is with your sister and only fucking you."

"You know what, fuck you! I'll move your shit back. You can do better than that and just move your shit out of my house."

"I'll be gone tomorrow." he told her then headed back to his room. He got his cooking kit out, grabbed the dope that he had gotten from Rocko and headed into the kitchen to cook it up. Felicia fell on her bed and cried herself to sleep.

Ricky cooked the dope up and was amazed that it all came back. He did not lose one gram, which indicated that the dope was good.

He cut up two ounces and stashed the other two inside of the mattress. He stretched out on the bed and let his mind start to drift. He fell asleep as thoughts ran through his mind.

π

Felicia woke up early the next morning. She left out of her room, and went to Ricky's. She seen that he was sleeping peacefully. She realized that she did not want him to move out. She really liked him and thought maybe she should have told him the truth from the beginning.

She was hoping that somehow he would forgive her. She walked over to the bed and climbed into it. She unzipped his pants, reached inside and pulled his dick out. She lowered her mouth onto it.

Ricky thought he was dreaming. He was sleeping and felt himself being aroused. He felt a warm sensation on his dick. He moaned from the pleasure that he was getting from it. He was dreaming that Felicia was giving him head, and it felt so real. When he felt himself about to cum he tried to wake up to prevent from having a wet dream. When he forced himself awake he found that it wasn't a dream, Felicia really was giving him head.

He looked down at her and she looked up at him as she hungrily continued to suck his dick. Ricky could not do nothing by lay there. The head that she was giving him had him paralyzed. The muscles in his legs started to stiffen, and his feet pointed forward as his cum started to erupt out of him like a volcano. His whole body shook. It was as if Felicia was a priest and she was performing an exorcism on him, sucking the devil out of him. When she finished he felt light-headed and fell back onto the pillow.

Felicia climbed up and laid her head on his chest. She used her fingers and made circles on it as she started talking to him.

"Ricky, I'm sorry, I know that I should have told you what was going on with me and Marcus from the jump. I hope that you can forgive me. I swear, I do care about you. I told Marcus that I cared about you and that he had nothing coming anymore. That is why he was mad and started taking things that he had bought for me back. I'm not a hoe. He was the only person that I was fucking. You been staying here, so you have seen for yourself that don't no niggas come over here or call here. I can be a good woman to you, just give me a chance. Don't say anything now, just think about it."

With that, she got up and left out of the room. Ricky just laid there, he had a lot of things on his mind, but one thing he knew was that he was not going to let anything come between him and his money. He got up, went and took a shower, then got dressed. He grabbed his work and left out of the house heading to the block.

8

Ricky's father had been feeling miserable. He had been real grumpy and his wife noticed how he had become withdrawn and quiet.

His wife tried to comfort him, "He's going to be okay Harry. Have faith in God, he will protect him."

"I'm a failure Marlene. Maybe I should have spent more time with him, than I did overtime at work. That's my boy, I could have did more."

"You can't blame yourself Harry. Ricky is a grown man now. He is not a boy anymore. You have nothing to do with the decisions that he decides to make."

"That may be true, but it doesn't take away the pain. I'm going out there to find him tomorrow. I'm going to try and talk to him. See if I can get him to come take a job at the mill."

"You do that, but don't put yourself up for a letdown. If he says no, you have to accept that." They got into bed, cut off the light and went to sleep.

π

The next day Harry talked his foreman into agreeing to hire Ricky at the mill. Now all he had to do was to convince Ricky to take the job.

When he got off of work, he headed up to the recreation center to see Smitty. He knew that Smitty knew everything that went on in the streets and that he could tell him where to find Ricky.

Smitty was inside of the ring, training one of his pupils, when Harry entered the gym. He looked up and seen Harry come in and told the kid to take a ten minute break.

He climbed out of the ring and approached Harry, "How is it going Harry?"

"Not too good, I have been feeling real down lately."

"You look like you have been having a rough time. It's Ricky isn't it?"

"Yeah, it's him. The boy done moved out of the house and is out in them streets full time. I figured that you might be able to lead me to him so that I can talk some sense into him."

"I here that he be over there on Outhwaite hustling. They say that he done even bought himself a car. He's been moving real fast. He is going to be all in pretty soon."

"Not if I can help it!" Harry told him. He shook Smitty's hand then left the gym. He drove around the comer to Outhwaite.

When he got to the middle of the street he saw Ricky sitting on the hood of a blue Chevy. He pulled up behind the Chevy and parked. He got out of the car and walked to the front of the car that Ricky was sitting on. Ricky looked up and seen him but said nothing. Harry walked over and sat on the hood next to him.

"How are you doing son?"

"I'm good Pops."

"This your car?"

"Yeah, it's mine."

"Yo Ricky!" someone called out to him. Ricky seen that it was a customer and told his father, "Hold on for a minute Pops." he headed in the direction of the customer. They did their transaction right out in the open as Ricky's father watched.

Ricky walked back over and sat on his car.

"Ricky, you know that you don't have to be out here doing this. My foreman is willing to hire you on to the job."

"No thanks Pops, that's a slave's job."

"You think I'm a slave?"

"No Pops, but they work you like one for peanuts. I'm going to have more in the next year than you have had all of your life."

"There is nothing wrong with working hard Ricky. It's legal money that doesn't have repercussions that come with it. That poison that you are pushing only leads to death or prison. That fast money ain't going to last long believe me. Your uncle has been in jail for fourteen years messing with that heroin."

"I'm not uncle Mike, and I rather take my chances out here, than to work like a slave for thirty years and still have nothing." Harry started to shed tears as he realized that he had lost his son to the streets.

He walked back to his car and got into it. He set there for a minute thinking.

He blamed Marcus for introducing his son to the devil's poison, and had thoughts of finding him, and choking him until he had no more life in him. Harry drove home, went in the house and right to bed. He did not even acknowledge his wife, who sat up waiting for him to come home to let her know how things had gone with Ricky.

She could tell from his actions that things had went bad. She knew that she couldn't possibly tell him that the school had called her, telling her that Terresa had been missing too many days of school. She figured that she would have to deal with that situation on her own.

π

The next day, while Harry was at work all he could think about was how he should have spent more time with Ricky. He was working really hard to provide for his family, but he realized that it did not leave him with time to spend with his children.

He wondered how him not spending time with Terresa was effecting her. He was scheduled to work over time that day, but he went and cancelled it. He figured that he would get off at his regular time and go pick Terresa up from her drama class and take her out to dinner.

π

Harry got off of work at four o'clock and drove up to the rec center. He went down to the bottom floor where the drama class was held. He entered the room and seen several kids up front performing. He scanned the room of spectators looking for Terresa, but did not see her.

Mrs. Ferguson saw him standing in the back of the classroom and headed towards him.

"How are you doing Mr. Henderson?" she asked him while she stuck her hand out. He reached out and shook her hand.

"I just thought I would stop by and pick Terresa up and take her out to eat."

Mrs. Ferguson put a confused look on her face, "I'm sorry to tell you this Mr. Henderson, but Terresa hasn't attended this class in over a month. I have been wondering if she was coming back, seeing as she never cleared out her locker."

"I don't know what's going on with these kids of mine. I did not know that she was not attending these classes. That means that I have just been giving my money away. I will make sure that she is here tomorrow Mrs. Ferguson. You have my word on that."

"She is always welcomed Mr. Henderson and her presence is missed. I will look forward to seeing her." Harry left the center and went home. He stormed up to Terresa's room, but she wasn't there. He went into his room, where his wife was sitting on the bed reading a newspaper.

"Marlene did you know that Terresa hasn't attended one drama class in over a month?" Marlene then knew that it was bigger than her missing school and that she needed to let him know what she knew.

"No, I did not know that Harry, but the school did call me yesterday and told me that she has been missing an excessive amount of school days."

"Why didn't you inform me Marlene?"

"You have been going through so much with Ricky, that I figured that I would just handle it myself."

"We are losing a grip on our children. I wonder what would make that girl miss school and drop out of her drama class. We should have paid more attention to them. They have been deceiving us right under our noses. We are going to get to the bottom of what's going on with her tonight." Harry said to his wife.

They sat up waiting on Terresa to come home. It was after midnight when she got into the house. She walked into the living room and was startled when a voice called out in the dark, "Where the hell have you been!" The living room light flicked on and she seen her mother and father sitting there on the couch.

Terresa was high as a kite. Her and Tone had been smoking crack for most of the day. She tried to compose herself and get a lie straight in her head, "I was over to Kim's house doing my homework."

"That's funny, because your mother got a call from the school yesterday telling her that you haven't even been going to school. I dropped by your drama class today and found out that they have been getting free money from me, because you haven't been there in over a month." Terresa stood dumbfounded. She could not even think of anything to say.

"What do you have to say for yourself?" her father asked her as he got up off of the couch and started to approach her. She just stood there as he approached her. She was too high to be scared, and as he got close to her he noticed that her eyes were glazed over. He stopped and stared at her. He looked her up and down and realized that she had lost a considerable amount of weight. He took in the fact that her clothes hung loosely off of her.

Harry breathing became labored and his body started to swell up. He grew up around people that did drugs and could easily recognize the symptoms of people that were on them. He raised his hand high in the air and brought it down with so much force, that when his hand connected with Terresa' s cheek she went flying off of her feet. She flew into the wall and slid down it.

"Harry! What the hell is wrong with you?" Marlene asked him as she jumped up off of the couch.

"She is on drugs Marlene! She is high right now!" he said as he went to advance on her. Marlene hurried over to him and grabbed him.

"She is a girl Harry. You can not hit her like that!"

"What the hell am I supposed to do Marlene. We are losing our kids. Ricky is grown, she is only sixteen years old. You telling me that I can not discipline her?"

"You can not be hitting her with your hands."

"Okay! I will use my belt!" he told her and started removing his belt. Terresa begged to her mother, "Don't let him hit me mommy. I'm sorry I swear I won't do it anymore!"

"I'm going to make sure of that!" Harry told her as he raised his belt and brought it down striking her on her legs. Terresa yelled out, "Please stop daddy!"

"It's too late for all of that. You should of thought about that before you started messing with that poison. You got to pay for your devilish ways!" he said to her as he struck her with the belt again.

Terresa sprung to her feet and took off towards the steps with her father on her heels. He hit her in the back with the belt two times before his wife grabbed a hold of him.

"That's enough Harry!" Harry stopped and turned to his wife. The look that he had on his face scared her. She had never seen him with that look on his face in all of the time that they had been together. She noticed that his whole body was shaking. She started rubbing up and down on his arm trying to calm him down.

"She is going to rehab tomorrow. You let her know to pack her shit. You might as well get the phonebook out right now and start looking for rehabs!" Harry stormed upstairs to his room and slammed the door behind him.

Marlene went to Terresa' s room and entered. Terresa was curled up in a fetal position on her bed. Her mother sat on the end of the bed. She did not even know how to start the conversation. She had never dealt with those type of things before.

"Terresa," she called out to her. In between sniffles she answered, "What?"

"How did you end up on drugs?"

"My friends were doing it and I just wanted to fit in."

"If you have to change anything about yourself for somebody to accept you then they are not your friends. Your friends are going to accept you as you are. They are not going to push you to do something that you don't want to do. Especially something that will destroy your life. You and your brother do not appreciate the type of love that we have for you two. We have been sacrificing for years to give you the best opportunities to be successful in life, and you are set on throwing them away. What type of drugs have you been doing?"

"Primos and crack."

"Oh my God! Are you insane. I do not know what a primo is, that crack thing has been all over the news. It is causing a epidemic that is sweeping all over the country. They say that it is destroying whole families. You have to get help. Your father says that he is putting you in a rehab tomorrow."

"I don't need no rehab. I'm not addicted to it. I just won't do it no more."

"Your father is not going for it. He wants you to pack up some clothes. I agree with his decision. You say you are not addicted but your behavior is showing different. Hopefully it won't take that long for you to complete a program."

"What about school?"

"What about it? You haven't been thinking about it. They are probably going to provide classes at whatever program you get enrolled in." her mother got up and left out of the room. She went back downstairs and got the yellow pages and started looking through them to find some programs. She circled five of them, planning to call them in the morning, then she went upstairs and climbed into bed with her husband.

π

The alarm clock went off at 7:45 in the morning waking the Hendersons up for work. They got up and got dressed. Marlene went and started calling the numbers that she had circled. She decided to go with a program that was inside of Metro hospital, because it provided classes for kids that were still in school.

She went up to Terresa's room to tell her to get her things ready. When she opened her bedroom door, she found that the bed was still made and that Terresa was not in there. She knew that Harry was going to throw a fit. She went down to the kitchen where he was drinking a cup of coffee and told him the bad news, "She is gone

57

Harry." he slammed his fist down on the table so hard that it made the silverware and the saucer that was on it fly into the air.

"Dammit Marlene! You keep saving them from me and handing them right over to them streets. You should of just let me beat some sense into them!" he jumped up and headed towards the door. She called out, "Harry where are you going?"

"I'm going to ride around and see if I can find her. If I do I'm going to tie her down and drive her straight there."

"Let me get my purse, and I will go with you."

"That's okay, all you do is interfere, I got this!" he told her then left out of the house.

Harry rode around for hours looking for Terresa. He rode through all five of the projects. He even offered people money to give him her whereabouts. No one gave that information up, but he did find out that she had been hanging around some hustler that was up there from Detroit. They told him where he could sometimes find the guy hustling at. He drove to that area and began a stakeout.

New Flavor Books

9

Ricky hit the block with a vengeance. The fiends were loving his dope. He couldn't believe how his clientele was building up. Marcus was back to serving himself on Case Court, but most of his customers were going to spend with Ricky. He knew that he was going to have to do something about that situation real soon or he was going to be driven out of business.

He started thinking of a plan to get Ricky out of the way.

Ricky sold out on two ounces in one day. When he went in that night he did not even go to his room he headed straight to Felicia's room. She was up under her cover asleep. He stripped out of his clothes and climbed into bed with her. She only had on her panties and a bra.

He slid up behind her and took one hand to pull her panties to the side, while he used the other one to guide his dick into her. When his dick entered her, Felicia woke up fully. She put an arch into her back so that he could get further inside of her.

Ricky reached in front of her and pulled her bra up over her titties, letting them be free. He put both of his hands on them. He squeezed them as he fucked her from behind. Felicia reached her hand up over her head behind hers and started rubbing on Ricky's head.

Ricky rolled her onto her stomach and pulled her hips up. He started fucking her from behind. Felicia reached behind her and spread her ass cheeks apart giving him better access.

Ricky looked down and watched his dick going in and out of her. With her holding her ass cheeks apart, her asshole started to look inviting to him. He thought it winked at him. He bent down and spit into her asshole, then he stuck a finger into it. After it loosened up he stuck two, then three inside of it finger fucking her asshole. He pulled his dick out of her pussy and Felicia rose all the way up into the doggy style position. She knew what Ricky wanted and planned on giving it to him. She put her hands back behind her, to spread her cheeks back open. Ricky spit in his hand then rubbed it around the head of his dick. He put his dick at her asshole entrance and pushed in. Felicia grunted as his dick invaded her, but she did not try to run from it. She kept her position and held her ass cheeks open as he fucked her.

Ricky put his hands on her shoulders to pull himself all the way into her. Her ass was so beautiful to him. It was the color of a ripe banana. It rounded out perfectly in the position that she was in. He bent over her and started kissing her on her back. Felicia responded by telling him, "It's yours Ricky, get it baby. I can take it, fuck this ass." Ricky pulled out of her and roughly rolled her onto her back. He took her legs, put them together and pushed them back. Felicia wrapped her arms around her legs and pulled them further back. Ricky got on her and positioned his dick back at her asshole. The head popped in, then he sunk in until his nuts fit snuggly into the crack of her ass.

To Felicia, it felt like he was up in her guts. She could feel him in her spine. Ricky asked her, "Is this how you want it? Did Marcus give it to you like this?"

"Hell no! Marcus ain't got shit on you! You big dick mother fucker! You nasty mother fucker! Fucking my asshole like this?"

"You love it don't you?"

"Hell yeah nigga, do that shit." Ricky fucked her in her ass until he came. She thought that his nut had gone up into her stomach.

After they were through, they decided to take a shower together. After the shower they got back into bed and fell asleep with Felicia wrapped up in Ricky's arms.

π

The next morning Ricky was up bright and early ready to hit the block. Felicia got up and cooked him breakfast while he got ready. When he entered the kitchen, there was a plate with pancakes, scrambled eggs, bacon and grits. There was also a tall glass of cold orange juice. Ricky thought to himself, "I could go for this on the regular."

He ate the food, then told Felicia that he would see her later. He left heading for the block.

Ricky pulled up on the strip, and was surprised to see that there was a line of people waiting there for his arrival.

He was glad that he had taken a chance with Rocko. The way that things were going he was going to be through with the rest of the package that day. His only worry was that he did not have a number to reach Rocko at. Ricky thought to himself that he was going to have to find out more about the man who seemed to know a lot about him.

He finished up the pack by 11:30 that night. He was heading to his car, when out of his peripheral vision he saw someone coming across the street heading towards him at a fast pace. He quickly reached into his waist and pulled out the same twenty two pistol that Marcus had given to him. The figure had his hat pulled low over his face, and had his right hand stuffed inside of his jacket pocket. He seen Ricky about to get in his car and moved faster.

He called out to Ricky, "Let me holla at you for a minute." Ricky turned towards the approaching figure.

"What's up?"

"I'm trying to cop something."

"Shops closed, see me tomorrow."

"Hold up nigga let me holla at you!" the person said as he closed in on Ricky. Ricky did not wait for him to get around the back of the car. He just raised his arm and started firing the gun at him.

The figure was shocked that Ricky had a gun. He was told that it was going to be an easy lick. He found his self being shot at. He had to duck down and return fire as he turned and ran in a zig zag motion back to the way from which he had come.

Ricky quickly jumped into his car, started it and sped off. His heart was beating fast and he was sweating real hard. He had never shot a gun at anyone before. He thought back to what Marcus had told him, "People are always looking for a easy lick."

He figured that he had just proven to whoever it was that tried to rob him, that he wasn't an easy lick.

He went to the house, and counted all of the money up he sat aside thirty two hundred for Rocko and then counted out his profit. He made fifty five hundred dollars for his self. Putting that with the rest of the money that he had stashed, he had almost fourteen thousand dollars. He was fascinated at how much money he had made in such a short period of time.

Felicia laid there on the bed observing him. She had seen it in him. She knew that he could do big things.

Ricky's body was shutting down on him. All the ripping and running he had been doing along with the events that had just happened took its toll on him. He felt extremely tired. He stretched out and fell asleep with all of his clothes on. He slept until mid afternoon the next day. When he got up, he took a shower grabbed some money and left the house.

π

He drove over to the west side to check out a couple of car lots. He decided that he wanted a different type of car, a car that a lot of people were not driving. He pulled into an Audi used car lot. He traded in his Chevy with six thousand dollars and drove off of the lot in a 1983 Audi. The Audi was dark blue and had a power sunroof.

Ricky opened the sunroof halfway and cruised back over to the east side. He did not have anymore work, so he decided that there wasn't any sense in going up on the block. He thought that after what had happened the night before that it was probably hot anyway. He figured that he would go find him a bigger gun though.

He rode up to King Kennedy projects and located Shotgun. Shotgun was the number one supplier of guns down the way.

You could buy anything from a twenty two to a hand grenade, if the money was right. He sold Ricky a brand new looking .357 for

$350.00. Ricky liked how powerful the gun felt in his hands. He stuck the gun into his waist, got into his car and headed home.

π

Marcus found out, that the robbery did not go as planned and got mad as hell.

"Your stupid ass couldn't do a simple job." he said to the would be robber.

"Nigga, you ain't tell me that the nigga was going to be strapped."

"Don't worry, I'll handle the shit myself." Marcus told him.

10

Terresa had been staying with Tone. He was struggling to stay afloat. Tone had started smoking more dope than he was selling. His appearance was declining as well as his ambition to hustle. Sometimes him and Terresa would sit up in the house days at a time and get high.

Terresa had only took a couple of outfits with her when she left home. She found herself wearing the same clothes over and over.

One day Tone looked up and realized that he was broke. The rent on his home and car was coming up, plus Manky's sister was tripping because he did not give her any money for the rent and the car note.

He decided to sell some of his jewelry to get a package. The bad part was that he had to go to Rocko to get the package. Rocko had heard that he was smoking dope, and was glad at his misfortune.

When Tone came to him to trade his jewelry for some dope he started to snub him. He looked at him and felt sorry for him. He seen how broke down Terresa was looking, and he decided to help them in their decline. He gave Tone more than what he asked for the jewelry, knowing that he would be back anyway.

He told Tone, "You know that you are looking bad bro. Don't let that shit take you all the way under."

"I'm good, I'm about to take this pack and get back on my feet."

"If you say so," he then turned to Terresa, "I wonder what Ricky would do if he saw you looking like that?"

"How do you know Ricky?"

"Me and your brother are in business together. He did not tell her that Judy had put him on to Ricky. Tone and Terresa left. Tone went back to the house to package up the dope. Once he had it packaged, him and Terresa got back in the car and drove down to Unwin Drive, where he served often.

He pulled up on the strip and parked. Harry was glad that he hadn't given up. He had taken a two week vacation from work to case out that dope strip, in hopes of finding his daughter and the man that had her on drugs. He seen a car fitting the description that he had been given, pull up and park. He seen that it was two people inside of the car.

He went into his glove compartment and pulled out his .38 police special. He tucked it in his waist then got out of his car. Tone had gotten out of his car and was standing on the sidewalk. Terresa remained sitting in the car.

Tone noticed the huge, middle aged guy approaching and thought that he was about to be a new customer.

"What you need?" he asked Harry as he approached. Harry walked past him and up to his car. He looked into the car and seen Terresa, "Hey what are you doing old man?" Tone asked him. Harry swelled up with anger. He turned and quickly grabbed Tone by the throat. Tone took both of his hands and tried to remove the hand that was squeezing the life out of him from around his throat. Both of his hands could not remove the one hand that had a grip on his neck.

Harry threw Tone into the car and startled Terresa. He pulled out his gun as Tone slid down the car onto the ground. Terresa quickly jumped out of the car, "Daddy stop!" she ran around the car as her father was cocking the hammer back on his gun.

Tone was laying on the ground still trying to catch his breath, when Harry reached down and grabbed him by the collar. He put the gun to his forehead and told him, "If I catch you near my daughter again I will kill you! Do you understand me?" Tone could not do nothing but nod his head.

Terresa jumped on her father's back and started beating him in the back of his head.

"Stop it! You leave him alone." Her father reached behind him and snatched her forward. She flipped through the air and landed onto the ground. He turned towards her and went to snatch her up. When he turned Tone jumped up off of the ground and went at him.

He grabbed the arm that Harry held the gun in. The jerk on Harry's arm caused him to squeeze the trigger, and a bullet tore through Tone's shoulder.

"You shot me!" Tone said as he fell to the ground.

Terresa ran over and knelt down beside Tone. She had tears running down her face. She turned to her father and screamed.

"You are a animal!" Harry heard sirens in the distance and knew that someone must have called the police.

He reached down and snatched Terresa up. She started kicking and yelling as he carried her to the car and put her into the front seat. He strapped the seat belt on her, then locked and shut the car door. As soon as he walked around to the driver's side, Terresa started trying to unhook herself.

Harry got into the car, started it and then pulled off. While he was driving the passenger's door flew open. He had to stop the car and reach over her and pull the door shut. He held onto her with his right hand as he headed for Metro hospital.

π

Tone pulled himself up and got into his car. He started it and tried to drive off, but because of the pain in his shoulder it was hard for him to steer the car. He drove down the street swerving. When the police turned onto the street they saw the car driving erratically. They pulled behind Tone with lights flashing.

Tone knew that he had dope on him and wasn't trying to go to jail. He hit the gas trying to get away. He flew down Central Avenue, all of a sudden he lost control of the car and it went across the lane and hit an oncoming car head on.

The police surrounded and approached the car. Tone's eyes were closed and his head was laying on the steering wheel, but he was still breathing.

The driver of the other car was not as lucky. He died from the impact. When the paramedics removed Tone from the car, the police searched it. They found the drugs, so he was facing drug charges, fleeing and eluding as well as an involuntary manslaughter charge.

π

Harry took Terresa to Metro Hospital's residential drug program. The program was located on a secure floor, so he did not have to worry about her leaving. He signed the necessary paperwork and she was admitted. Two orderlies had to drag her kicking and screaming to her room. Harry left hoping that his daughter would be alright. Now he needed to figure out how to get through to his son. He headed home to get some much needed rest.

/ /

Ricky pulled up on the block the day that he was supposed to meet Rocko. He sat low in his car because he did not know if his attacker from the other night would try again.

When he seen the Maxima pull pass him he blew his horn. Rocko kept driving slowly down the street. Ricky pulled out and got behind him blowing his horn repeatedly. Rocko pulled over and quickly jumped out of his car with a gun in his hand. Ricky pulled over behind him and got out with his hands raised.

"It's me man," he said to Rocko.

"Shit, I ain't no who you were I was looking for the Chevy."

"I had to switch up after somebody tried to run up on me." Rocko immediately thought that Ricky was about to try and hit him with a sob story.

"So, you got jacked?" he asked him with a smirk on his face.

"Some fool tried to jack me, but I sent him back in the direction that he came. Here go your money right here." he handed Rocko his money.

"So now what's next?"

"You got some money on you?"

"Yeah, I got some money."

"Okay, follow me then." Ricky got back into his car and followed Rocko over to Longwood. They parked in a parking lot on 33rd and entered an apartment building. They reached the third floor and Rocko opened the door to the apartment. When they entered the apartment they could hardly breathe. It was as if someone had just gotten through cooking a whole kilo of dope. The people in the house jumped up and started scattering.

Rocko seen that Frank, Slim, Micky, Coo Coo and Rita were all smoking crack.

He blew his top, "What the fuck! You niggas are smoking dope? You niggas are smoking up my shit with these bitches. Now I know why my shit has been coming up short." Ricky stood there observing the scene. He recognized the two girls as being his sister's friends. He knew that his sister hung with them regularly and wondered was she too getting high.

Rocko went on a war path. He pulled out a gun and started smacking the women and pistol whipping the guys.

"You bitches are going to work off the money that you smoked up. You niggas might as well pack your shit up. You two are going back to the D. I can't have no crack head mother fuckers rolling with me. I'll have to kill you niggas. Get your shit, I'm taking you back today."

He turned to Ricky, "Come with me." Ricky followed him into a back bedroom. They went inside of the room and Rocko closed the door.

"So how much do you have on you?"

"I got thirty two hundred."

"Look, I got a quarter key left, so you buy a eighth and I'm going to front you the last one that I got. I got to take these crack head mother fuckers back to Detroit and I can't leave shit in this crack head hoe's house. When I get back I got to find my own spot. I can't keep shit here no more. I will just see you in four days same as before, is that cool?"

"Yeah, that's a bet," Rocko gave Ricky the quarter bird and he left. Rocko had Slim and Frank put their things into his car and he drove them back to Detroit. He had intentions of bringing back a whole new crew.

π

Ricky drove to the house. He put up one of the eighths and cooked up the other one. He bagged it up and figured that he was going to have to find a better way to hustle. He needed to be able to stay mobile, so that he would not be a stationary target for people that wanted to rob him. He left the house and drove to a pager shop. He bought two pagers, one for him and one for Felicia. He figured that he could page her and have her bring him work when he ran out instead of having to travel way back home to get it.

He went back home and tossed Felicia the pager.

"What is this for?" she asked.

"I will tell you, right now grab your purse, let's go."

"Where are we going?"

"To get you a car?"

"A car, I don't have no license."

"Don't worry you will get that next."

Ricky drove over to the west side and put a down payment on a Chevy Celebrity. They went to the BMV and Felicia took the written driving test. She passed and was given her temps. She followed Ricky back to the house.

When they got there Ricky started teaching her about dope. He showed her how to tell the difference in the size of a pack. He showed her from an eight ball up to an ounce. Then he told her, "That pager that I gave you is for me only. When I page you, I'm going to tell you what type of pack to bring me and where to meet me at.

"Just cause you got a car don't have your ass out just kicking it. Do your thing, but always be around somewhere close in case I need you, you got that?"

"Yeah, I got it."

"Alright, I have to hit these streets." he told her then left back out of the house.

Ricky went back down to the projects. He pulled up on the strip and got out. His customers started coming out of the woodwork. Ricky started serving them and giving them his pager number at the same time. After that day he was no longer just going to post up on the block. He was going to ride around and make sales off of his pager. He had even decided to sell a little weight. He started passing out his pager number to other hustlers on the block, telling them that he was selling anything from fifty dollar dubs up to ounces. He figured that with his new plug that he could step his game up.

His clientele rose quickly. By selling weight he made less of a profit, but he had a quicker turnover rate. By the time that Rocko had came back from Detroit, which was two days later, he was ready to reup. He still had not gotten a number for Rocko, so he went back over to the apartment that Rocko had taken him to. When he pulled into the parking lot, he seen that Rocko's car was there. He smiled, grabbed his money and got out of the car. He went upstairs and knocked on the door and Rocko opened it.

"What brings you by so soon?" he asked Ricky as he let him in.

"Money," Ricky said as he stepped in. He tripped out when he seen his sister's two friends down on their knees giving two dudes that Ricky had never seen before head.

"Money you say?" Rocko asked him. Ricky had to force himself to turn away from watching the girls, "Uh yeah, I need to reup."

"Nigga you got through with that shit that fast."

"Yeah, I'm done, I'm trying to straighten you out and buy a quarter bird."

"That's what the fuck I'm talking about, get that paper. Roger, Tookie, this is Ricky. You two need to take notes from this nigga. He ain't faking like them crack head ass niggas Slim and Frank." Roger and Tookie both gave Ricky head nods as they continued to get head from the girls.

"Come on into the back Ricky." Ricky followed Rocko down the hallway. They entered the same room as before and Rocko went to a closet and grabbed a gym bag. He sat the gym bag onto the bed and unzipped it. He poured its contents out onto the bed.

Ricky's eyes got big as he saw all the kilos of cocaine roll out of the bag. He had only seen that much dope on TV in the movie Scarface.

"I told you that I'm tired of pushing little weight Ricky. We can get rich together. You can put niggas on the blocks on, and sell all weight, it's your choice." Ricky paid him his money then gave him enough to purchase a quarter of a key.

"I will be back at you soon." Ricky told him as he put the dope inside of his shirt and turned to leave out of the room. He remembered that he did not have a number for Rocko. He turned back towards him, "Aye, I need a number to reach you at?"

"Okay, I'm going to give you my sky pager number. I found me a spot out in Maple Hts, but I'm still going to be stationed down here. You can roll through at any time, I fuck with you Ricky, niggas like you are hard to come by. You be careful out there, you are coming up real fast and people are going to start to take notice. Once that happens they are going to come at you all types of ways. They are even going to send bitches at you, so stay on your P's & Q's."

"Good looking," Ricky told him then left out of the apartment. He headed to the store. He needed to get some bigger bags and a bigger scale, because he was about to enter into the big leagues.

12

Teressa had been in rehab for over three weeks. She had worked her way down two levels, meaning that she was going to start getting passes to leave outside of the program for a couple of hours. The first pass that she got was a group pass. A group of patients were given a pass to go and help serve dinner at a soup kitchen. It was to show that they could be responsible.

One of the program's sponsors was the group leader. Once they got to the center the sponsor assigned everyone their duties. Terresa was put on the serving line. She was serving soup and halfway through the meal she asked to be relieved so that she could go to the restroom. She was relieved by one of the other patients. She was given directions to the bathroom. She headed into the bathroom. She closed the door and looked around hoping to find a window.

The bathroom was windowless, so she crept out of it. She walked down the hall until she came upon a door. She tried the knob and the door was unlocked. She opened the door and seen that it was an office. She stepped inside, closed the door and locked it. She went over behind the desk and pulled back the curtain. Through the window she could clearly see the street. She turned the lock on top of the window, unlocking it. She pulled the window up then climbed out of it. When her feet hit the ground she took off running.

She ran about three blocks before she decided to slow down to catch her breath. She did not have any money at all, so she decided to thumb a ride. After about twenty minutes of walking and holding up her thumb, someone finally pulled over and offered her a ride. A middle aged white man picked her up.

"Where are you on your way to sweetheart?" he asked her after she had gotten into the car and closed the door.

"I'm going over to the east side."

"What are you doing out by yourself, are you working?"

"What do you mean am I working?"

"You know, are you working the streets?"

"You mean prostituting, hell no!" The man got nervous, "Calm down sweetheart. I did not mean any harm." Terresa settled down.

"How old are you?" the man asked her, "I'm sixteen." All thoughts of trying to get her to have sex with him went out of his head when she told him her age. he wished that he had never picked her up. He drove her quickly over to the east side. She had him drop her off at Tone's apartment. When she got out of the car, she seen that all of Tone's things were sitting on the curb. She walked up to the door and seen that it was an eviction notice attached to it.

She knew then that Tone must have still been in jail. She could not think of anyplace to go. She was cold and hungry, but more than anything she was fiending for a hit.

She crossed her arms as she prepared for the trek down to Longwood. She walked from 120th and Buckeye down to 30th and Community College. She entered the apartment building and went up to the third floor. She knocked on the door and Rocko opened it. It took him a minute to recognize that it was Terresa.

The last time that he had seen her she was looking bad. She stood at the door with her weight back up and a glow on her face.

"What brings you down here?" he asked her.

"Tone is in jail and I have no place to go."

"What has that got to do with me, I ain't your man. I ain't fucking you."

"Can you just give me something?"

"Ain't nothing in this world free. You want something you got to work for it. If you are ready to work come in." Terresa hesitated then entered the apartment and Rocko shut the door behind her. She saw Coo Coo and Micky sitting on the couch and there was two guys that she had never seen before.

Coo Coo and Mickey jumped up, ran over and gave her hugs.

"Where you been girl?" Micky asked her.

"My father had me in rehab."

"For real? How did you get out?"

"They gave me a pass to go help at a soup kitchen and I jetted."

"Bitch, you're crazy."

"Enough of that, this ain't no reunion. Head on back to the bedroom." he told her.

"Can I get something first?" Rocko pulled out a twenty and tossed it to her. She did not know what to do, because she did not have a pipe to smoke the dope out of.

Micky, who was fiending for a hit pulled out a stem and told her, "Here you can use this," Terresa went over and sat between Micky and Coo Coo. Micky reached into her pocket, pulled out a lighter and handed it to Terresa. She put the crack into the stem and fired it up. She sat there and smoked with her two friends until nothing but air came through the pipe.

"Bitch ain't shit else in there. Come on let's go to the bedroom." Terresa got up and headed down the hall. She waited outside of a closed door until Rocko walked up and opened the door. They both entered and Rocko told her.

"Take all of your clothes off. I see you got your weight back. Let me see how that body looks." Terresa started stripping off her clothes. When she was standing before him naked he told her, "Come here, I see that ass is looking fat again." Terresa walked over to him and he reached around her and grabbed a handful of her ass cheeks. His dick got rock hard as he thought about fucking her young ass. He went over to the dresser and grabbed a jar of grease, then walked back over to her, "Bend over the bed." Terresa walked over to the bed and bent over putting her hands on the bed. Rocko walked up behind her and undid his pants. He dropped his pants and drawers down to his ankles, then he opened up the jar of grease. He scooped some out and started rubbing it on his dick.

Terresa was wondering what he was doing, so she looked behind her. She seen him greasing his dick up and knew what he was about to do. She quickly turned around and sat down, on the bed making sure that he couldn't get to her asshole.

"Fuck is you doing!"

"I don't do that!"

"Bitch you are going to do what I want you to or you can put your shit on and get out."

"Let me give you some head?"

"Fuck that! I want what's precious to you."

"Is you going to go slow. I ain't never did that before."

"Don't worry I got you." Terresa got back in the position and he took his hand and put it to her asshole rubbing grease on it. He aimed his dick to the entrance of her asshole and pushed in. Once the head opened up her hole he put his hands on her hips, to pull himself into her. The pain became so unbearable to Terresa that she held her breath until she almost passed out. She should not have told Rocko that she was a virgin back there, because he loved inflicting pain on people. Soon as his dick was halfway in her. He started banging her. He did not go slow nor give her time to adjust. He went at her like a wild animal on its prey. Every time Terresa would fall onto the bed, he would snatch her back up.

He kept fucking her until he started to smell something foul. He looked down and seen that his dick was covered in shit. He instantly lost his cool and struck Terresa in the back of her head. Terresa fell onto the bed crying, "I'm sorry,"

"You nasty bitch!" he yelled at her. He pulled up his pants, then snatched her up. He threw her with force onto the other side of the bed. Her head hit the end of the night stand, and Rocko heard a loud thud. Terresa crumbled to the floor and laid still. Rocko walked around the bed and yelled at her, "Get up bitch!"

He reached down to pull her up and her body was completely limp. He started shaking her trying to get her to wake up, but it was no use. Everyone out in the living room heard the commotion. Tookie walked back and knocked on the door. The knocking startled Rocko, who yelled out, "What!"

"Is everything cool in there?"

"Yeah, everything is good. I will be out in a minute."

"Okay bro!" Tookie said then went back up front.

"What's going on back there?" Coo Coo asked him.

"They are just having rough sex that's all. I could go for getting my dick sucked right now." he said as he walked over in front of Coo Coo and started unzipping his pants.

In the bedroom, Rocko was in panic mode. He was praying that she wasn't dead. He put his ear down to her nose trying to hear if she was breathing and heard nothing.

He put his hand in front of her nose, but he felt no air coming out of her nostrils. He started to panic, trying to figure out how to get rid of her body.

He knew that he could not do that with her friends sitting around the house. He left out of the bedroom, closing the door behind him and walked up to the living room. He saw that Coo Coo was giving Tookie head. He cut it short, "Aye, they got to go, we got to make a move right quick!"

"Just let her finish, bro."

"Nigga, they got to go now!" They all looked at Rocko and could tell that something was going on. He looked very nervous and was sweating. Micky asked him, "Can we wait on Teressa?"

"Terresa is about to help me take care of something. She will see you later, come on!" he told them as he went over to the door and opened it. They both got up and walked past him out of the door. When they both walked past him, they noticed that he smelled like shit.

"Damn did you smell that?" Coo Coo asked Micky.

"Yeah, that nigga smelled like shit. That ain't the only thing that smells foul though. He ushered us out of there for a reason. Something must of happened that he don't want us to know about. We are going to lay out here and see what's up. Matter of fact let's go down to Pam's house. That is where Rita is at."

They both went down to the first floor apartment and knocked. Pam let them in and Micky told them that it was something funny going on upstairs and that Rocko had kicked them out.

Back upstairs, Rocko went into the kitchen and grabbed a roll of duck tape out of the drawer. He went back into the living room and told Tookie and Roger to come with him. They followed him to the bedroom and when he opened the door a foul smell hit both of them.

"Damn nigga! What happened?" Tookie asked him when he seen Terresa lying on the floor.

"It was an accident, I need y'all to help me get rid of the body."

"Nigga, I came up here to hustle not to catch no murder case!" Roger told him.

"All you got to help me do is get her out to the trunk of my car and I will take it from there!" he said to them as he began snatching the sheets off of the bed. He laid them out on the floor.

"Tookie grab her legs and lift her up when I lift her arms up." Tookie grabbed her legs and lifted them, while Rocko lifted her upper body. They placed her on the sheets and wrapped her up in them. Rocko taped the bottom, middle and top of the sheets. He then gave Roger the keys to his car and told him to go out to the car, make sure that the coast was clear and to pop his trunk.

Roger left out of the house. For a minute he had thoughts of just taking off. He did not want to have anything to do with what was going on. The only reason that he stayed was because he did not know his way around Cleveland and did not have a way to get back home.

He went outside and looked around. He did not see anyone, so he went over and opened up the trunk.

Rocko and Tookie carried the body out of the apartment and down the stairs. When they got to the exit they called out to Roger and he told them that the coast was clear. They quickly exited the building, heading to the car.

Rita, Coo Coo, Micky and Pam all watched from Pam's kitchen window as Rocko and Tookie carried what looked like a body wrapped in sheets to Rocko's car and put it in his trunk.

They stuffed the body into the trunk, then Roger headed back upstairs he wanted no parts of helping them to get rid of the body.

Tookie got into the car with Rocko. They had put a lot of work in together back in their hometown and he wasn't going to turn his back on him. They drove out of the Longwood projects and drove up to King Kennedy projects. Rocko thought that if her body was found, up there that the police would think that the crime had occurred up there.

They pulled into a parking lot that had a big green dumpster sitting at the end of it. Rocko turned the car around and backed it up to the dumpster. He got as close as he could and had the bumper touching the dumpster. He opened up the glove compartment and hit the button that popped the trunk then him and Tookie exited the car. They both walked to the back of the car. They had to lift the body up from standing on the sides of the car. They lifted the body up out of the trunk and threw it inside of the dumpster. They, then jumped back into the car and pulled off.

Rocko turned to Tookie, "That nigga Roger is making me nervous. Do I got to worry about him running his mouth?"

"Roger can hold his water. He just don't want to be caught up in no bullshit that don't add up to nothing. He is about paper and anything that he does has to be related to getting paper."

"Mistakes happen and when they do you have to deal with them."

"Rocko, people have to deal with their own mistakes."

"This was your mistake not Roger's."

"Yeah, but if he is down with me, then he is down through whatever."

"That's your opinion. Like I said, you have nothing to worry about. Me and Roger have done much dirt and none of it has came to light."

"I'm going to take your word, but if that nigga gets to acting funny, I'm going to handle my business." Rocko told him as he drove heading out to his house in Maple Hts. He needed to take a bath and calm his nerves. He pulled a primo out, lit it and smoked it as he drove.

13

The next morning an old man named Leroy, who collected cans to turn into the scrap yard, pulled his shopping cart up to the dumpster. He grabbed his stick that had a magnet on the end of it and climbed over into the dumpster.

He started tearing opening garbage bags in search of cans. As he was bent over going through a bag he lost his footing and fell. As he was falling he put his hand out to catch himself. He fell onto his butt and his hand landed on a hard object. He took his hand and started feeling the object. To him it felt like a face wrapped in some type of clothing. He turned over onto his hand and knees and moved the trash bags that were on top of the object. He seen that whatever it was it had tape around it. He removed his pocket knife and cut the tape off. He opened the end from which he had cut the tape off. He scrambled trying to stand up, but fell several times as he tried to get out of the dumpster. Even though the eyes were still open on the face, he was quite sure that the girl was dead.

He started yelling for help and screaming as he finally got out of the garbage bin.

"Call the police! Help! Help!" a guy that was coming out of his apartment building on his way to work seen Leroy making a big scene. He called over to him, "What the hell is wrong with you old man?"

"There is a dead body in the dumpster! Call the police!"

"You're tripping, ain't no damn body in there!" The man said as he walked over to the dumpster. He got over to it, climbed up and looked over into it, "Oh shit!" he said as he jumped back down to his feet. He ran back into his house and called 911. He told them that it was a dead body in a dumpster outside of his building.

Within twenty minutes several police cars and paramedics arrived on the scene. Yellow tape was used to secure the area until the crime lab could get there to collect evidence.

After the crime lab removed the body from the dumpster and collected the evidence, the coroner took the body, while homicide detectives questioned Leroy and the man who had called them. The detectives got all of the information that they could, which wasn't much, then headed over to the morgue to see if they could identify the victim and find out how she had died.

π

The rehab had notified Harry that his daughter had skipped out on the program, and he was furious. He blamed the people who ran the program, for allowing her to be able to leave so fast. He had been back out in the streets looking for her, but had no luck. He even went back up on Outhwaite looking for Ricky. He knew that Ricky cared about his sister and did not want her out there running the streets and doing drugs. He drove up and down the strip for two days, but did not see Ricky nor his car. He had no idea that Ricky had gotten a different car and was no longer selling dope on the block.

Harry was starting to lose it. He had no more vacation or sick days, they had all been used up dealing with his children. He was starting to sleep lesser and lesser. What his kids were doing was troubling him very deeply, and he was starting to think irrationally.

His wife steady tried to comfort him, but it was no use. He kept sinking deeper and deeper into depression.

It was 7:30 in the morning and Harry and his wife were up getting prepared for work, when they heard a knocking at the door.

"I will get it," Marlene called out as she headed down the stairs.

"I'm coming," she called out to whoever it was that had kept knocking on the door. She got to the door, opened it and was surprised to see two white men wearing suits standing at her door. The first thing that came to her mind was that Ricky had gotten himself into trouble.

"May I help you?" she asked the two men.

"Are you Mrs. Henderson?"

"Yes I am!"

"Is your husband home also ma'am?"

"Yes he is, may I ask what this is all about?"

"Mrs. Henderson I am detective Roberts and this is detective Mackie. We are from the homicide division and would like to talk to you and your husband."

"Homicide! Oh my God! Has something happen to Ricky?"

"What's going on?" Harry asked as he came down the stairs.

"Harry they are from homicide. Something must have happened to Ricky!" she said and started crying. Harry became choked up as he descended the stairs.

"Mr. Henderson it may be best if you and your wife took a seat so that we can talk to you."

"I don't need to sit down, whatever you have to tell us just say it." He told the detectives as he became more choked up.

"Mr. and Mrs. Henderson it saddens me to have to tell you this, but there is a body of a teenage girl who has been identified through dental records as Terresa Henderson, down at the county morgue."

"No! ... No! It can't be! Harry it can't be!" Marlene yelled as she crumbled to the floor. Harry reacted violently he swung his fist as hard as he could into the wall. His huge hand went through the plaster breaking two of his knuckles at the same time. His hand throbbed but he felt no pain. No physical pain could compare to the mental and emotional pain that he was feeling. He laid his head against the wall and began banging his hand on it.

Detectives Roberts and Mackie had been through the scene that was before them many times before, but never had they had to tell a family that their 16-year old daughter was found dead in a garbage can. They both had daughters themselves, so the murder of the young girl had affected them also. They understood that you needed to stay professional at all times, but what human being would not be affected by the senseless death of a child.

Roberts walked over and helped Marlene off of the floor. He led her over to the couch, where she flopped down and continued to sob.

"Mr. and Mrs. Henderson I know this is a devastating time but we need one of you to take a look at this picture to identify the body." Roberts said to them as he held the photo in his hand.

Harry got his self together and walked over and took the photo out of his hand. He looked at the photo and was crushed. His baby girl was lying on a slab. The right side of her face was bruised and swollen. He could tell that she had died a violent death.

Tears started flowing freely down his face. He handed the photo back to Roberts telling him in between sobs that, it was her in the picture. Marlene did not even attempt to look at the picture. She could not bare to see her little girl dead.

"What happened to her?" Harry asked them.

"It seems that she died from blunt force trauma to her head. She was found in a dumpster naked and her body was wrapped and taped in a sheet. The coroner has ruled it a homicide. I promise you that we will do everything in our power to catch the person that is responsible for her death and bring them to justice."

The only justice that Harry wanted to see was the death of the person that had killed his baby girl. He wanted to take justice into his own hands, not wait, on law enforcement and the judicial system to hand it down. He decided that, he wasn't going to wait for them to find the killer, he was going to find whoever it was his self.

14

Later that day the murder was all over the news and crime stoppers were offering up to $5,000 for anyone with any information leading to the arrest of whoever was responsible for the death of Terresa Henderson.

Judy's television was on as she sat up in her room doing her homework. Her father had come down hard on her for missing school and staying out late. After they had placed her in the detention center for a week, she straightened out. She had stopped hanging out with her friends, and no longer was messing with Rocko. She knew that Micky and Coo Coo were still hanging around him. They no longer even went to school anymore.

She was horrified to see her friend's death on the news. She started feeling bad, because she realized that it was her that had introduced Terresa to drugs. Before Terresa got on drugs she was a sweet innocent young girl. Drugs had turned her into a totally different person. Judy thought that had Terresa never ended up on drugs that she would surely still be alive.

She started to wonder how Micky and Coo Coo were doing out there in the streets, and if they had heard about what happened to Terresa.

π

Felicia heard about the murder on the news. She did not know if the girl was related to Ricky, but she knew that she shared his last name.

When, he came in that night she told him what she had seen. Ricky was sitting on the bed counting out money, when she told him.

"Ricky they had on the news earlier about some sixteen year old girl with the same last name as yours being murdered."

"I'm not the only person in the world with my last name. What was the girl's name?"

"It was Terresa, I think." Ricky's body went stiff.

He dropped the money onto the bed turned towards Felicia and quickly grabbed her around the throat. He started choking her, "Bitch! What type of games are you playing?" Felicia's eyes were bulging out of their sockets. She slapped at Ricky's arms trying to get him off of her.

When Ricky seen that her face was turning red, he let her go. He went around the room grabbing all of his things. Felicia did not know what was going on.

"Ricky … Ricky … What's wrong baby?"

"Bitch! You are playing deadly games, telling me that my sister got killed."

"I did not know, that she was your sister. You never told me your sister's name or that you even had a sister. I only told you because of the last name."

Ricky was confused, "Shit! Shit! Shit!" he said to himself. He sat down on the bed for a minute, then jumped right back up and ran over to the phone. He picked the phone up and dialed home. His father answered the phone in a dry voice and he could hear his mother crying in the background. He knew then that it had to be true. He still needed confirmation.

His father spoke into the phone, "Henderson's residence."

"Pops is it true?"

"Ricky it's true. Your sister is gone. I told you son that them drugs only lead to jail and death. You wouldn't listen and she wouldn't listen. Now my baby is gone."

"I'm on my way over there Pops?"

"Ricky, I told you that as long as you are selling that poison, you are not allowed to step foot into this house."

"I want to see mom, Pops."

"See her at the funeral." he told Ricky then hung the phone up on him.

Ricky was crushed. His sister was only 16 years old. He couldn't figure who could possibly want to do harm to her. He thought back to seeing his sister's friends sitting up in Rocko's dope house.

When he seen them in there, he knew that they were under age and shouldn't have been up in there. He felt it was none of his business. He wondered if someone had seen his sister sitting up in someone's dope house but thought the same as he did, that it wasn't their business.

He went over and put his arms around Felicia, who was sitting on the bed crying.

"I'm sorry!" he told her as he pulled her to him and held her tightly. They cried on each other's shoulders.

Six days later was Terresa's funeral. It was packed with family and friends, even Judy was there. Ricky was there with Felicia at his side. His father did not let him, ride in the limo with them, but he was allowed to sit up front with them during the service. He sat next to his mother and kept his arm around her. His father did not pay him any attention. He sat there with his hand in a cast.

Once the funeral was over, Terresa's body was carried out to the Hurst. There was a funeral procession to the cemetery. Everyone stood around as the preacher gave last rights, then she was lowered into the ground. After Terresa was in the ground, everyone got into their cars, and headed down to the Henderson's for a funeral reception. Marlene told Harry that she wanted Ricky there.

"He's my only child left, I'm not going to turn him away."

"You have him if you want to, but tell him to stay out of my way." They all went to the Henderson's house to eat dinner and to celebrate the life of Terresa. Ricky mingled with his family and friends. He tried his best to stay out of his father's way.

Ricky thought that since he was there that he might as well pick up some of the things that he had left when he moved out.

He went upstairs and was heading to his old room when he heard whimpering coming from his parents room. The door was only halfway closed, so he stuck his head inside of it. He seen his father sitting there on his bed crying. He pulled his head back and went to his old room. He took a pillow case off of one of the pillows and started putting his things into it.

He looked around his old room one more time then walked out. He was walking down the hallway on his way back downstairs. When he was passing his parents room. His father called out to him, "Ricky come in here for a minute." Ricky walked into the room and his father patted a spot on the bed next to him, indicating for Ricky to take a seat. Ricky went over and sat next to his father.

His father sat there crying, just looking at Ricky.

"What's up pops?" Ricky asked him.

"I just wanted to tell you, that I have nothing against you son. I'm only against what it is that you are doing, I love you Ricky. God knows I love you, but I can not take you out in them streets selling that poison. I hope that you get your life together and if you do you are always welcome back here."

"Thanks Pops," Ricky told him then gave him a hug. They embraced for a long time. When they broke the embrace, Ricky went downstairs and said his goodbyes. He hugged his mother, then him and Felicia left heading home.

Rick drove in silence and Felicia sat staring out of the window. They were both trapped in their own thoughts.

Felicia was taking in the fact of how dangerous the streets had become since the emergence of crack. Ricky was thinking about how having money did not necessarily make you happy. He thought, "Yeah, I'm buying material things, but not being with my family is leaving me with a void feeling. I have pushed the ones that truly care about me away." He thought about having Felicia, "She says she cares about me, but is it really me that she cares about or the money that I'm making?"

He started to wonder if it was all worth it. He realized that he had not had any peace since he had entered the drug game. The altercation with his father, the bumping heads with Marcus, having to shoot a gun at someone and the biggest thing, the death of his little sister.

Ricky battled with his conscience as he drove. With all of the things that he had realized, he still came to the conclusion that he was going to continue to hustle, at least for the time being.

When they got to the house, they went straight to their bedroom. Ricky went to the closet, pulled out a gym bag and went and sat on the bed. Felicia took off her high heeled shoes and headed to the bathroom to remove her make up.

Ricky unzipped the bag and dumped its contents out onto the bed. Stacks of money fell out of the bag, and he began unwrapping it so that he could count it.

While Felicia was in the bathroom she was thinking to herself how Ricky was going through a rough time. She knew that he was battling with his conscience. She was one of the few people who understood that selling drugs was as much an addiction as actually doing them. Most people that sold drugs were addicted to the lifestyle that came with it and no amount of money ever seemed to satisfy them. She felt that what most drug sellers did not realize was that selling drugs was a hustle and that hustling was just that, hustling.

People that were good at hustling drugs could be good at hustling anything. They could hustle legally and still live a nice lifestyle. She decided that she was going to bring that fact to Ricky's attention.

When she reentered the bedroom, Ricky had the whole bed covered in money, "How much is that?"

"Fifty five thousand," he told her.

"You know that you can invest that money. You can buy a house to rent out, open up a restaurant or a store."

"It's going to take more than this to do something. You got to keep putting money into a business before you start seeing a profit.

I'm going to need at least another fifty thousand as back up before I can think about doing something like that."

"Ricky most guys that sell dope set goals only to keep moving them back every time they reach them. Don't be like the average drug dealer and keep fooling yourself by setting goals that you are not going to keep. What you are doing is not something that you can do forever without experiencing some repercussions. You are going to do what you want, but now is the time that I must tell you, I'm seven weeks pregnant. You are going to be a father."

"What! Why are you just now telling me this? I don't even know if I am ready to have a child." he was upset and started stuffing the money into the bag without even wrapping it back up.

"I been wanting to tell you. You have been ripping and running the streets so much, that I haven't actually had a chance to tell you."

"That's bullshit! And you know it. I'm here every night, we fuck, we get up together, you meet me out in the streets. You have had plenty of times that you could have told me."

"That may be true, and I'm sorry that I did not tell you sooner. The fact still remains that I am pregnant and is about to have your child."

"That's a fact that remains to be seen." he told her as headed out of the room and left the house.

Ricky jumped in his car and took off driving nowhere in particular. He just wanted to ride around and clear his head.

π

Back at the house, Felicia heard a knock at the door. She knew that Ricky had just left. She wondered had he forgotten his keys.

She went to the door and opened it. As soon as she unlocked it, the door was kicked opened. The force sent her falling onto her behind. Two masked men entered the house with guns drawn. One of them walked over to her and smacked her in the face with the gun. The other man closed the door and said, "Bring her into the room!" Felicia immediately recognized that voice as Marcus'.

The man drugged her by her hair following the other man into the bedroom.

"Where the money at bitch?" the man asked her as he drug her across the floor. Felicia started screaming for help and the man quickly shut her up by striking her in the mouth with his pistol. Felicia felt two of her teeth break loose.

The man that she knew was Marcus went straight to the closet and after rambling through it for a few minutes he came out with the gym back, "Jackpot!" he said to the other man. He walked over to Felicia and raised his gun, "Call the police about this bitch!" he told her then shot her at pointblank range in the face.

The other robber was startled. He knew they were about to commit a robbery, but he wasn't told anything about committing a murder, "What the fuck! Nigga you crazy! Let's go!" The two men hurried and left the house.

When they were turning off of the street, Ricky was turning onto the street. He had only ridden around for about twenty minutes before he realized that he was overreacting.

Having a kid should have been good news to him. It also would give him a foundation. He decided to head back home and apologize to Felicia.

He pulled up and got out of the car. He was approaching the house and seen that the door was partially opened. He thought for a minute and was sure that he had closed the door when he left. He got to the door and pushed it open. He called out, "Felicia! Felicia!" but he got no answer.

He was mad that he did not have his gun with him. He crept to the bedroom and seen that the door was closed. He turned the knob and pushed the door opened and found Felicia sprawled out on the floor. Her face was covered in blood. He surveyed the room and seen that the closet door was opened.

He knew that it had to be a robbery. He went and knelt down next to Felicia. He could not tell if she was dead or alive. He knew that if she wasn't dead and he tried to call and wait for a ambulance that she would die for sure.

He picked her up in his arms and carried her out to the car. He put her into the back seat, climbed into the front seat and took off heading for the hospital.

He pulled up to Kaiser Hospital's emergency room parking lot. He got out of the ear and opened the back door. He pulled Felicia out of the back seat and carried her into the emergency room. Once he was inside of the sliding doors, he started yelling, "Help! Help! I need Help!"

The nurse that was sitting behind the glass counter looked up and seen that he had a girl whose face was covered in blood in his arms. She called for two orderlies to bring a gurney and she hit the call button, notifying the emergency room doctor that they had an emergency.

"This way sir!" the nurse pointed towards the orderlies that were moving fast towards them with the gurney. Ricky headed in their direction meeting them. They took Felicia out of his arms and rushed her into one of the trauma rooms.

The nurse asked Ricky, "Sir do you know what happened to her?"

"I think she has been shot!"

"Sir I'm going to need you to take a seat until the police arrive. Whenever there is a shooting or a violent crime we must notify the police."

"Do whatever you have to do, but save her. She is carrying my baby."

"We will do the best that we can sir!" The nurse told him, then left to enter the trauma room.

The doctor was in there giving out instructions. Felicia was alive with a weak pulse and they were trying to stabilize her. She was hooked up to an IV and a respirator. Her face was cleaned off and the doctor could see the bullet's entrance and exit route. The bullet entered Felicia's right cheek and exited right under her left ear.

Fortunately, the bullet did not cause any major damage. At most her mouth was going to have to be wired shut for six to eight weeks.

The doctor had her prepped for surgery. Her cheek bone and her jaw were broken. The nurse informed the doctor that there was a possibility that she was pregnant and he ordered that test be done to determine if in fact she was pregnant and had any harm been done to the baby.

The pregnancy test came back positive and further testing confirmed that the baby was okay and that there were no more complications.

Ricky sat out in the waiting room. He was waiting to get the word on Felicia's condition as well as to talk to the police when they arrived.

The police arrived first and the nurse pointed Ricky out to them. Rick was sitting in the waiting room with his head down when the officers approached him.

"Excuse me sir," Ricky looked up and seen two plain clothes officers standing before him.

"Yes,"

"Are you the person that brought the injured young lady in?"

"Yes sir,"

"What is your name?"

"Ricky Henderson,"

"What is the victim's name?"

"Felicia Harrison,"

"Okay, my name is detective Michaels and this is detective Smith. We would like for you to step outside with us so that we can ask yon a few questions."

"No problem sir," Ricky followed the detectives outside and the questions began.

"Do you know who shot Ms. Harrison?"

"No I do not,"

"Were you with her when she was shot?"

"No,"

"Where were you when she got shot?"

"I was riding around in my car."

"Riding where?"

"I was just riding around."

"May I ask why you were just riding around?" Ricky started to get frustrated by all the questions, "Look, today was my sixteen year old sister's funeral. She was killed and put into a dumpster by some animal. After leaving the services and my parents home Felicia hit me with the news that she is pregnant. I decided to go for a ride to clear my mind."

"How long were you gone?"

"About twenty minutes."

"So, you left the house for twenty minutes to drive around and get your thoughts straight."

"Yes,"

"And when you went back, you found Ms. Harrison where?"

"She was lying on the floor in the bedroom."

"You have no idea as to who shot her and why?"

"No, I don't!"

"Mr. Henderson we are going to need you to take us to where the crime occurred, so that we can look for any clues that may lead us to who shot Ms. Harrison." Ricky figured that there was nothing there that he had to worry about, since he had been robbed of everything.

"Do you want the address, because I want to stay here until she comes out of surgery?"

"We need someone to give us entrance to the house."

"The door is unlocked." Ricky gave the detectives the address and they headed to their car. When they got into their car and were heading to the address, Smith called for forensics and back up to meet them at the scene.

When they arrived at the scene two police cruisers were already sitting in front of the house. The crime lab hadn't made it there yet.

The detectives got out of the car, with Michaels going to the trunk of the car. He went into the trunk and pulled out an evidence kit. The kit contained a finger print duster, an ultraviolet light and some latex gloves. He also pulled out a flashlight and turned it on. He put on a pair of latex gloves and handed Smith a pair.

The other officers had got out of their cars and joined them in the driveway. Michaels pointed the flashlight at the ground as they headed up the driveway, looking for clues. When they reached the house he dusted the door and door knob for prints. While dusting, he noticed that the door did not have any damage done to it.

"Whoever entered must have been let in because there is no sign of forced entry." he said to the others.

"We will have to check all of the windows before we can come to that conclusion." Smith informed him.

"Yeah, I guess you're right." After he finished dusting for prints, he turned the knob and opened the door. Just as Ricky had told them the door was unlocked. They all filed into the house and started looking around. They spread out throughout the house.

Michaels turned on the ultraviolet light, after he seen what appeared to be a spot of blood two feet away from the door. He knelt down, "Smitty come take a look at this," he called out. Smith went over and knelt beside him under the light, they could see a trail of blood spots. Staying crouched down, they followed the trail, which lead them into the bedroom.

Once inside of the bedroom, they came to a pool of blood in front of the bed.

"This is where he must of found her." Michaels said.

"The assault must of started out there in the living room, but it's apparent that she was shot in here." Smith said.

"Why would they bring her in here?" Michaels asked the question out loud.

"Maybe they were looking for something." Smith said and started looking around the room.

He seen that the closet was open and walked over to it. When he got to it, he seen that someone had been rummaging through it. Clothes and shoes were scattered all over the floor.

"They were definitely looking for something. The question is did they find it." Smith said then stepped into the closet. He squatted down on the floor looking under the scattered clothes and shoes. After finding nothing he stood up and started checking the shelf. There were a lot of shoe boxes up on the shelf and he started pulling them down and opening them up. He finally came upon a box that seemed too heavy to be holding a pair of shoes. He pulled   the box down and lifted its top, "Michaels take a look at this."

Michaels stopped rummaging through the nightstand drawer and walked over to Smith. He looked inside of the box and seen what appeared to be dope. Right then two guys from the crime lab entered the room, "Good evening gentleman." one of them said to Smith and Michaels.

"You two are late but, your right on time. We need you to test this and see if it's what we think it is."

"Sure, I will just have to take it out to the van." Smith told Michaels.

"I will go out there with him, while you keep searching. I think we have found the motive already. Most likely it was a robbery."

"That is what it seems like." Michaels agreed with him. Smith and the crime lab technician left to go out to the van to test the substance.

Michaels continued his search of the room and upon flipping over the mattress he found a .357 magnum handgun. Finding dope and a gun led him to believe that Ricky was a drug dealer.

The other officers had searched the rest of the house and had come up with nothing. They found that none of the windows had been breached neither. They joined Smith and the crime lab unit out in the driveway.

Michaels walked outside, carrying the gun in a plastic bag.

"Look what I found under the mattress." he called out to Smith.

"Looks like that is going to be an additional charge for Mr. Henderson, because this has tested positive for cocaine. It is pure cocaine at that."

"We better head on back to the hospital, before Mr. Henderson decides to bail."

All of the officers and the crime technicians got into their vehicles. Michaels had the two patrol cars follow them to the hospital to make the arrest on Ricky.

The doctor was in the waiting area talking to Ricky. He was explaining to him, that they had to perform reconstructive surgery on her cheek and had to wire her jaw shut for six to eight weeks. He informed Ricky that she could probably be released from the hospital within a week.

Ricky was preparing to ask the doctor some follow up questions, when he noticed the two detectives that he had talked to earlier approaching him. They had four uniformed policemen with them. He noticed that the police all had their gun holsters unstrapped and had their hands on the butts of their guns.

Detective Michaels pulled out a set of hand cuffs when he got within reach of Ricky. He reached out and grabbed Ricky's arm, "Mr. Henderson, you are under arrest for possession of cocaine and the possession of a firearm. You have the right to remain silent. Anything that you say can and will be used against you in the court of law."

Ricky interrupted him, "Fuck all that! What am I being arrested for, I ain't possessing shit!"

"There were drugs and a firearm located inside of your home."

"What home? I don't have a home."

"We will work that out down at the station." he told him as they led him out to their car.

15

Rocko had been paranoid ever since they had placed Terresa's picture all over the television. What really had him spooked was that they were advertising a five thousand dollar reward for any information leading to the arrest and conviction of the killer.

He thought to himself that he was glad that he had made them little crack head hoes leave before he had gotten rid of the body. He had taken Roger back to Detroit after they had gotten into it about what had taken place. He had brought another guy name Marco back to join him and Tookie.

He figured that he was in the clear, even though he was still feeling nervous. Tookie told him, "Maybe you should go back to the D until things cool down up here."

"Ain't no way I'm taking all of that dope back to Detroit."

He was wondering why he hadn't heard from Ricky. He attributed it to him mourning over the death of his little sister. He thought to himself, "Damn, I will be glad when that nigga get over that bitch's death, so he can get back to spending that money." Ricky was his biggest customer and things were going slow without him.

Rita and Pam were sitting in Pam's kitchen fiending and scheming. They had smoked up all of the dope that Rocko had given her for the day and were trying to figure out how to get some more dope out of him.

"Rita, I know he done seen that girl's death on the news. He has got to be scared, with there being a five thousand dollar reward out."

"So, what you want to call crime stoppers and get caught up in that mess. You know that it's a trick talking about giving up five thousand dollars. That's why they say up to five thousand dollars."

"Bitch! I ain't thinking about calling no damn crime stoppers. I say we tell him that those little girls have been going around running their mouths. Telling people that they think Rocko, killed that girl. Shit, he might give us an eight ball for that information."

"You want to go upstairs and tell him?"

"No, you need to go up there and get him to come down here. We don't want to talk to him in front of his boys."

"Okay," Rita said to her then left Pam's apartment.

She went upstairs to her apartment and went inside. When she walked in Rocko was sitting in a chair smoking a primo and his two partners were sitting down watching TV.

Rita walked into the kitchen then called out, "Rocko let me talk to you for a minute."

"Rita, I ain't giving your fiending ass no more dope. You get four stones a day that's it."

"This ain't about no dope, this is important." Rocko got up and walked into the kitchen, "What's so important?"

"Me and Pam would like to talk to you downstairs about some-thing important."

"I know you old hoes ain't trying to get me to trick with y'all?"

"Rocko, quit playing, this is serious."

"Fuck you need me to go downstairs for? Why she couldn't come up here? You bitches trying to set me up?"

"Rocko we are trying to tell you some serious shit, that we don't want to say in front of other people."

"Alright, lead the way." Rocko followed Rita downstairs to Pam's house. Rita knocked on the door and Pam opened it letting them in. When they entered she closed the door behind them and locked it.

"So, what's up?" Rocko asked them. Pam spoke, "we just wanted to let you know that them little young girls have been going around spreading rumors on you."

"What type of rumors?"

"They have been going around telling people that they think that you had something to do with their friend's murder."

"Why would they think something like that."

"Shit, I don't know, but they been saying that they watched you put what looked to be a body in your trunk." The hairs on the back of Rocko's neck stood up, when Pam told him that. He knew that he had to keep his cool.

"I have no idea why them hoes are spreading lies on me. I ain't worried about it. I haven't done no shit like that. Good looking though." he told them then turned and headed towards the door.

Pam called out to him, "Rocko!" he stopped turned and said, "What's up?"

"You aren't going to give us a little something for putting you up on game?"

"You ain't put me up on shit, because I haven't did shit!" he told them then left out of the apartment.

"I should call crime stoppers on his petty ass!" Pam said to Rita.

Rocko figured that had he given them something for the information, that it would of been like confessing to the crime.

He did not even go back upstairs instead he jumped into his car. He drove around looking for a hardware store.

He found one down on 55th and Central. He went in there and bought a jar of rat poison, then he headed back to Rita's.

When he got back, he went into the kitchen and cooked up a hot shot. He mixed a half a spoon of rat poison in with a fifty of cocaine. He cooked it up into a large rock, then he cut it up and put it into a vial. He labeled the vial then headed out to the living room.

"Tookie, I need you to ride with me right quick. Marco, you stay here and serve anybody that comes through."

Him and Tookie left out of the apartment and headed down the stairs. Tookie knew that something was bothering him by his body language.

"What's really up?" he asked Rocko.

"Them two little young bitches have been running their mouths. I got to find them and give them a hot shot."

"You know where they are at?"

"Them little bitches got to be around this hood somewhere. I'm going to ride until I find them. I know they got to be looking for a hit and I got one for them." Rocko rode through Longwood projects looking for them. He drove up on all of the strips, but saw no sign of them. He decided to drive up to the Longwood Plaza, which was also considered a strip.

He was driving through when he spotted the two girls leaving out of the Sav-Mor supermarket. They were walking and he pulled up alongside of them and rolled down his window.

"What's up with you two?" he asked through the window. Both of the girls looked at him but had different reactions to seeing him.

Micky was fiending and looking at him as the source of her next hit. Coo Coo on the other hand, got instantly scared. She saw a murderer and wanted to get as far away from him as she could. Rocko noticed that she was carrying a large grocery bag in her hands.

"You two trying to kick it and ride with us?"

"We have to take her mother her groceries back." Micky told him.

"Get in I will give y'all a ride. Me and my boy are trying to get a little head, you know I got y'all." he said to them then pulled out the vial of dope and shook it so that they could see it. Micky started walking towards the car as if she was hypnotized. Coo Coo refused to go with them, "I got to help my mother do something. Sorry I can't go."

Micky climbed into the back seat and told them. "I will do both of you." Rocko really wanted to get both of the girls together. He did not want to cause a scene by trying to force the girl into the car, so he decided to deal with the one he had for now and get the other one later.

He pulled off with Micky in the backseat. She pulled her pipe out, "Can I get a hit right now?"

"Sure," Rocko told her then tossed the vial back to her. She caught it and then looked in amazement at all of the stones in it. All excited she asked Rocko, "I can have all of this?"

"That's all you! Knock yourself out so that we can get this party started." Micky was glad that Coo Coo did not come. She was going to be able to smoke all of the dope by herself. She figured that it was enough to carry her into the next day.

She pulled her lighter out of her pocket. She put a nice size rock into the pipe and lit it. She waited for the pipe to fill up with smoke, then put it to her mouth. She took a strong pull and started coughing. The dope put a funny taste in her throat. She thought that it was something that he had cut the dope with. She took another pull and started to feel funny. A numbness started in her throat, then it seemed as if her jaw was becoming locked up. The next thing she knew, it became hard for her to breath. She started fighting for air and foaming at the mouth. Rocko watched her body start going into convulsions through the rearview mirror. He kept driving, heading down to the graveyard behind the King Kennedy projects. Micky was already dead in the backseat when they pulled up to the cemetery. Rocko pulled into the cemetery and drove halfway through. He pulled over and got out of the car. He opened the back door and pulled Micky's body out. He threw her to the ground, got back into the car and drove off heading to a car wash.

16

Marcus was feeling good about the lick that he had hit on Ricky. They had hit for $55,000.

Marcus only gave his accomplice $10,000, so he had forty five thousand to himself. He took pride in bringing Ricky up only to take him back down. He said to himself, "That's what happens when you bite the hand that feeds you." He did not have any regrets. He was living with Felicia's sister and felt no type of remorse for what he had done. To him both her and Ricky got what they deserved. He wondered when Felicia's sister would be notified of her death. He was ready to put his acting skills to the test.

Ricky had been booked for possession of drugs and having a firearm without a permit. The detectives questioned him about the things that were found and tried to get him to confess to knowing what happened to Felicia.

They told him that they knew that it was his drug dealing that led to her being shot. Ricky just sat there listening to them, but he would not agree to anything that they said.

After they seen that they were not getting anywhere with the questioning, they took him back to his cell. He was arraigned the next day and his bond was set at $20,000.

It took Ricky two days to get up the courage to call his parents. He decided that he would have a better chance with his mother than he would with his father. He called to his parents house collect and luckily his mother answered the phone. She accepted the call, "Ricky, tell me that you are not in jail?"

"I wish that I could tell you that ma, but unfortunately, that is where I am at."

"They caught you selling that stuff didn't they?"

"No ma, someone broke into the house and shot Felicia. The police were searching the house looking for clues, and found some drugs and a gun."

"Somebody shot that poor girl?"

"Yes, and she is pregnant with my baby. I need to get out to make sure that she is okay."

"That girl is going to have my grandbaby?"

"Yes ma,"

"Ricky, Lord knows you need to get your life together. You are bringing harm to your child before it has even taken its first breath. What is wrong with you?"

"Ma, can we talk about that after you get me out? My bond is $20,000, but you can get me out for $2,000 through a bondsman. I promise that I will pay you back."

"Ricky, the only promise that I want you to make is that you are going to get your life together."

"You got that ma,"

"No, I don't got that. I want you to mean it Ricky, or so help me God I will let you rot in there. At least I know that you will be safe in there."

"Ma, you have my word. I need to be out there for Felicia right now. I got the number to a bondsman. All you have to do is call him and make arrangements."

"Give me the number. I have to go to the bank. I will call him and see where he wants me to meet him after I pick up the money." Ricky gave her the number then asked, "So, I can count on you?"

"Ricky, I am your mother you can always count on me, just like you can always count on the Lord."

"Okay ma, I will be waiting." Ricky told her then hung up the phone.

Ricky's mother went rambling through her dresser drawer, looking for her checkbook. She could not find it and called out to her husband, "Harry have you seen my checkbook?"

"No, how much money do you need?"

"$2,000,"

"Damn Marlene! Why do you need that much money?"

"I have to go and bail Ricky out of jail."

"If Ricky is in jail, then you need to leave his ass in there until he gets some sense."

"His girlfriend was shot. She is in the hospital and is pregnant with his baby."

"That is why he should stay where he is. That boy is living a dangerous lifestyle and is going to bring harm to all those that are around him."

"Harry, I'm not going to leave my boy sitting up in jail. He gave me his word that he is going to get himself together, and that is all I need to hear." she continued to look for her checkbook. She found it under the clothes in her bottom drawer. After that, she called up the bondman and made arrangements for him to meet her down at the police station.

Her and Harry left the house at the same time, only they had different destinations. Harry was going out into the streets to try to find out anything that he could about his daughter's murder. He had been calling the police everyday looking for answers. They had yet to find out anything that would lead them to the murderer. The detectives had even started dodging Harry's calls. He decided then that he would investigate his daughter's death, find the killer and get justice. He did not want judicial justice, he wanted his own type of justice.

He had flyers made and went all through Longwood and King Kennedy asking residents if they had any information concerning his daughter's death. He knew that what he was doing was a long shot, but he was determined to put his all into what he was doing. He felt that he owed Terresa that.

π

Marlene went to the bank and withdrew $2,000, then she headed to the police headquarters in downtown Cleveland. When she got there, the bondsman was waiting for her in the lobby. She paid him the money and signed the necessary paperwork, then he went and paid Ricky's bond. It took them three hours to process Ricky out.

His mother had to call into work for the second time. On the first call she informed them that she would be in late. On the second call, she had to inform them that she would not be able to come in that day because of a family emergency.

She waited until Ricky was released. When he came into the lobby, they gave each other a hug, then Ricky told her that he needed her to take him up to the hospital to see Felicia. They headed out to her car and she drove up to the hospital. Ricky was relieved that when they got there, he found that his car was still parked in the same place that he had left it.

His mother parked and they got out and entered the hospital. The receptionist told them the room number and the floor that Felicia was on. They got on the elevator and headed up to her room.

When they entered the room, Felicia's bed was lifted up in the back, almost putting her in the sitting position.

It hurt for Ricky to see her laid up there with a tube in her nose and an IV in her arm. Her eyes were open and she turned her head in their direction when they entered her room. Because the surgery and her mouth being wired shut, she could not say anything. She could not even make any facial expressions. Ricky's mother started shedding tears as she watch the girl that was carrying her grandbaby lying up in the hospital bed like that.

She walked ever to the bed and grabbed Felicia's hand. She squeezed it and told Felicia, "You are going to be alright. God is going to take care of you." Felicia looked at her and tears started flowing out her eyes also. Ricky stood on the other side of the bed.

He needed answers. He needed to know who it was that had come into her home and did that to her. He took his hand and rubbed it through her hair as he looked down at her and asked, "Licia, who did this to you?" Felicia raised her hand, indicating that she needed to write it down.

Ricky turned to his mother, "Ma give me a pen and a piece of paper." His mother went through her purse and pulled out a pen and a piece of paper. She handed it to Ricky and he handed it to Felicia.

Felicia wrote on the paper and handed it back to Ricky. Ricky looked at the paper and his nostrils started flaring. "I'm going to kill that nigga!" he said angrily. His mother got worried, "Ricky, you let the police deal with it honey."

"Fuck that!" Ricky yelled as he headed out of the hospital room. "Ricky! Ricky! Where are you going?" his mother yelled after him. Ricky kept going. He caught the elevator downstairs, left out of the hospital and jumped into his car. He was so angry that he did not even realize that he did not have anything. He was going after someone who had tried to kill the girl that was carrying his baby, without a weapon. To anybody else they would of seen it as being suicidal.

Ricky was feeling invincible at the time. He flew down to the projects. He turned onto Case Court and could see the back end of Marcus' car parked at the curb down by the end of the street. Marcus was standing outside of his car leaning on the trunk talking to a girl. Ricky headed in their direction picking up speed. By the time they looked up Ricky was only two feet away from them. The girl moved quickly, but Marcus was like a deer caught in a car's headlights. He did try to pull himself up onto his hood right before the impact, but his left ankle and foot got crushed in between both of their bumpers.

The pain from his ankle being crushed was so unbearable that he almost went into shock. He opened his mouth to scream but no words came out.

Ricky did not even back up. He threw his car into park and jumped out. He jumped up onto the hood of his car and walked across it to Marcus' trunk. He reached down and grabbed Marcus' shirt collar and lifted him up. "You want to hurt a woman? You think your a man by trying to kill a woman? Why you ain't see me nigga, huh?

This how a man do it!" he told him then started punching him in his face.

He beat Marcus until he was lying on his trunk unconscious. Ricky's hand was swollen and bruised by the time he was tired of pounding Marcus' face. He decided to see if he could recover any of the money that he had lost. He went into Marcus' pockets and removed all of the money he had, along with his keys and wallet. He went through the wallet and found nothing but a driver's license. He put that and the other things into his pocket, but he was not satisfied with what he found. He went back to his car, got in, threw it in reverse and backed it up. Marcus slid to the ground with his foot hanging twisted at an awkward angle. Ricky threw his car back in park and got out. He went back over to Marcus' car and put the key into the trunk and opened it. Inside of it he found about an eighth of rocked up dope and a forty five automatic.

He still was not satisfied, because he had not recovered one forth of what Marcus had taken from him.

He looked around and took in the fact that there was a large crowd out there watching and knew that someone had probably called the police. He jumped into his car, pulled out Marcus' license and headed to the address that was listed for him.

When he got to the address, he pulled into the driveway, and got out of the car. He walked up onto the porch, and pulled the keys that he had taken from Marcus out of his pocket and started trying to find the one that opened the lock. He tried five of the keys, before he found the one that fit the lock. He entered the house and headed upstairs in search of the bedroom. At the top of the stairs was a bedroom that had the door open. He looked inside and could tell that it was a kid's room, so he kept going. When he came to the next room, there was a canopy bed and women's clothing scattered on the floor. Ricky entered the room and started rummaging.

Karen had just gotten out of the shower. She was drying off and could have sworn that she heard someone in the house. She figured Marcus must of came home and thought that maybe she could get a quickie.

Marcus had been neglecting her a lot lately and she wanted a nut. She walked out of the bathroom completely naked, heading to the bedroom. The door was pulled shut and when she opened it she became face to face with Ricky holding a gun in his hand. She used her arms to try and cover herself, as she looked around and seen how he had ransacked the room.

"What the hell are you doing Ricky and where is Marcus?"

"I'm looking for my money and Marcus should be on his way to the hospital."

"You better give me a better explanation than that or I'm calling the police!"

"Go ahead and call them. Tell them you are trying to protect the man that tried to kill your sister!"

"What the hell are you talking about?"

"You are so dumb, Marcus was fucking Felicia, for the longest and for some sick reason he thought that he could hook me up with her, and still keep fucking her. It must of been a coincidence that your sister decided to stop fucking him at around the same time that I chose to stop fucking with him. Marcus decided to kill two birds with one stone. He waited until I was gone and went to the house and robbed Felicia. He took a black gym bag out of the closet that had my money in it. To top it off, he shot your sister in her face. Miraculously she survived. She is laid up in Kaiser Hospital."

Karen stood there crying. She did not know how to feel. There it was Ricky was telling her that her sister was lying up in the hospital shot in the face, yet all she could think about was that he told her Felicia was fucking Marcus. She was more mad about hearing that Marcus was fucking her sister than she was about hearing that he had shot her.

She thought back to earlier in the week, when Marcus had come into the house with a black gym bag and went down into the basement. She realized that what Ricky was saying had to be true. She wanted to punish Marcus as much as she could. The bag is down in the basement somewhere." she told Ricky then sat on the bed crying.

Ricky left out of the room and went downstairs. He walked into the kitchen, spotted a door and opened it. He saw that it led down to the basement. He went down there and found that the basement was bare. It had no furnishings at all. He saw a wooden door that had a pad lock on it. He looked around the basement for something that he could use to break the lock. He spotted a shovel and went over and picked it up. He went over to the door and started beating on the lock with the shovel until the lock flew off. He opened the door and seen that it was some type of pantry, lined with shelves. On the top shelf he spotted his black gym bag. He pulled the bag down off of the shelf and set it onto the floor. He unzipped the bag and seen that it wasn't filled with as much money as he had left in it. He zipped the bag up, then picked it up and headed upstairs.

From the weight of the bag he could tell that quite a bit of the money was missing. He left out of the house, got into his car and headed home.

π

Karen got dressed, grabbed her car keys and left the house. She was heading up to Kaiser Hospital to pay her sister a visit.

17

The cemetery's caretaker had discovered Micky's body the day after it had been dumped. The same detectives that were called to the scene when Terresa's body was discovered, were at the scene. Detective Mackie wondered did they have a serial killer on their hands.

"Roberts this girl is about the same age as the other one, and was found only two blocks away from the last one. Do you think we have a serial killer on our hands."

"It is possible, but we have to take in the fact that the first girl's body was hidden. This one was left out in the open. Also the other girl died from being hit with some blunt object, but this girl has no signs of any physical injuries, therefore we can not jump the gun. We have to wait for the coroner's report."

And that is what they did. Two days later the coroner reported that Micky had died from poisoning. They found, traces of Arsenic and cocaine in her system. Mackie read the report and started thinking. He came to the conclusion that someone had intentionally poisoned the girl. The question that he needed answers to was who and why.

"Hey Roberts, why do you think that someone would intentionally poison a young girl like that?"

"Either they are sick or they wanted to make sure that she couldn't talk about something."

"You think that maybe she could have knew something about the other girl's murder?"

"It is a lead, that we can follow up on."

"All we have to do is find out if they were connected. If they were friends or even associates."

"We can do that by questioning their parents."

"Let's go," Mackie told Roberts. They were heading to talk to Terresa's parents and Micky's parents. They drove to Terresa's parent's home first.

Harry was there and they showed him a picture of Micky and asked him if his daughter knew her, "This here is one of Ressa's friends. What is she missing or something?"

"No Mr. Henderson, she is not missing, she is dead!"

"My God, that little girl is dead. What the hell is going on?"

"Mr. Henderson, we believe that she may have been killed because she may have had information about your daughter's killer. It seems that this girl was on drugs, the same as your daughter. We need to know if there is possibly another friend of theirs that could possibly be out there. If so she may be in danger and we need to get to her." Harry thought to himself.

"I don't want them to catch the killer. I want to catch him myself." He decided to keep the names of her other two friends to himself.

"No, I do not know of any other girls that she hung around. That there one is the only one that I ever met."

"Thank you for your time Mr. Henderson. If you think of anything else that could possibly help us, please contact us." Mackie told him then handed him his card. They left and Harry got dressed he was going to pay Judy and Coo Coo a visit.

π

Coo Coo wondered why she had not seen Micky since the day that she had gotten into the car with Rocko. She feared for her friend, but did not know who to turn to.

She thought about telling her mother, but realized that she would have to tell her things that she did not want her mother knowing about herself. She decided to go and talk to Judy. She went over to Judy's house and knocked on her bedroom window. Judy went to the window, seen who it was and opened it. Coo Coo climbed in.

She had to sneak her into the house, because her parents had forbidden her from hanging around Micky and Coo Coo, since she had gotten released from the detention center.

Judy was happy to see her friend and wondered where Micky was at, "Where is Micky?"

"I don't know, that is what I want to talk to you about. I think she might be dead."

"Girl! Why in the hell would you think that?"

"I think Rocko killed her."

"Why in the hell would Rocko kill Micky?" Coo Coo explained to Judy how they were at Rita's house one day and that Terresa came over. She told her that Terresa went into the back room to have sex with Rocko and that while they were back there something must of happened. She told her that they had heard what sounded like fighting, then everything got quiet. She explained to Judy how Rocko had come out of the room and told her and Micky that they had to leave. She told her that they had left, but had only went downstairs to Pam's house. She told her that her, Micky, Rita and Pam all had watched as Rocko and his friend Tookie put what appeared to be a body wrapped up in a sheet into the trunk of his car. Last she told Judy how two days earlier Rocko and the same guy had pulled up on her and Micky trying to get them to go with them. She told Judy how she made up an excuse not to go, but that Micky had gotten into the car and that was the last time she had seen Micky.

"If he was going to kill Micky, why would he let you go knowing, that you could give him up?"

"I don't know, maybe he knew that I was going to make a scene if he had tried to force me into getting in that car."

"Coo Coo, the things that you are saying makes no sense. I don't see Rocko being no killer. I was messing with him remember?"

"Yeah, I remember, I don't even know why I came here." Coo Coo said, then got up to leave.

"Hold on, look I will talk to Rocko and see what's up."

"Yeah right, like he is going to tell you that he killed two of your friends and is looking for the other one." Coo Coo climbed back out of the window.

She was heading home and could of swore that she saw Rocko's car trailing behind her. She took off at a fast pace running through the projects.

She ran all the way through Longwood and crossed over to the Outhwaite projects. She slowed up when she got by the rec center. She was walking when she seen a car turn onto the street and was about to take off running again until she seen that it was Ricky's car.

She ran out into the street and flagged him down. Ricky seen that it was one of his sister's friends and pulled to a stop. Coo Coo ran to his car and tried to open the passenger's side door. Ricky seen the frantic look on the girl's face and hit the switch to unlock the door.

Coo Coo jumped into his car, slid down in the seat and told him, "Just drive! Go!" Ricky pulled off, puzzled at the girl being so frightened.

"Coo Coo right?" he asked her.

"Yeah that's it."

"What's wrong, what are you so scared of?"

"Rocko is trying to kill me."

"Rocko!" he said shocked.

"Yeah Rocko! Ricky, I think he killed Terresa and Micky." Ricky looked at her like she was crazy. He hit his brakes hard, causing her body to be thrown forward.

"Have you been smoking more than crack?"

"Ricky, I'm serious, the last time that I saw Terresa she was down at Rita's house with Rocko. They went in the room to do something. After awhile we heard Ressa scream. Then everything got quiet. Rocko came out of the room and made me and Micky leave. We left, but we went downstairs to Pam's house. We all watched Rocko and his friend Tookie put what looked like a body wrapped in a sheet, into the trunk of his car.

A couple of days ago, Rocko and the same guy pulled uponme and Micky up in the Plaza. They tried to get us to get in the car and go with them. Micky got into the car, but I wouldn't go, and I haven't seen her since."

Ricky sat there thinking, he was in deep thought. All that Coo Coo was telling him, was too much to digest. He was trying to make sense of the things that she just told him. He hadn't seen Rocko since before he had gotten locked up. He knew that he was going to have to confront him. He figured that he would just page him like he wanted to get a pack then try to see how he reacted when he brought what she told him to his attention.

He turned to Coo Coo, "Have you tried calling Micky's house?"

"Micky ran away over a month ago. She hasn't been staying at home." Ricky was anxious to get to Rocko.

"Where do you want me to drop you off at?"

"Can I go with you? I have no place to go."

"I can't keep you with me. I got things to do." he told her as he pulled back onto Outhwaite. He pulled over and Coo Coo reluctantly got out of his car. She walked up to 40th and was about to cross the street to enter back into Longwood, when a car sped up along side of her and stopped. A man jumped out of the car and snatched her up, and threw her kicking and screaming into the backseat. He climbed in behind her, closed the door and pulled out a gun. He shot her twice in the head. The guy that was driving the car turned and told him, "Hit her one more time. Make sure she's dead." The guy shot Coo Coo in the head for a third time.

The driver drove across 40th and Woodland to the warehouse district. He drove down a hill that led to a bunch of factories, most of which were abandoned. They pulled into the parking lot of one, and pulled around back and parked where they could not be seen. Then the guy in the back of the car opened the door, got out and pulled Coo Coo's body out. He climbed into the front seat of the car and the driver pulled off.

18

Karen went up to Kaiser hospital. She needed to see her sister to find out what was really going on. When she entered Felicia's room, she became full of emotions. She was praying inside that what Ricky had told her wasn't the truth. Felicia's eyes were closed when she entered the room. She walked over to her bed and even though her sister was lying there in bad shape, she had thoughts of taking her hands, putting them around her neck and choking her.

She called out to her, "Felicia!" Felicia opened her eyes and looked into her sister's face. From the look on Karen's face, she could tell that she knew. Tears started to roll down her cheeks. That was confirmation to Karen, but she still had to ask her, "Is it true?" Felicia only kept shedding tears.

"Is it true Felicia? Dammit! Say something." Felicia took her hands and pulled open her lips showing Karen that her mouth was wired shut.

"Shake your head then dammit!" Were you two fucking?" Felicia shook her head indicating that they were.

"Do you love him?" Felicia shook her head no.

"How could you Felicia? How could you do that to me. I have been nothing but good to you. If you were not in that hospital bed I would kick your ass. Don't you ever speak to me again, in life!" she told Felicia then stormed out of her room.

She wanted to see Marcus suffer, so she called the police and told them that Marcus was the one that had shot her sister.

Marcus had pins and rods placed in his ankle and foot. He had just gotten released from the hospital, and was hopping towards the exit on a pair of crutches, when two detectives approached him. Detective Michaels spoke, "Marcus Ware you are under arrest for aggravated robbery and attempted murder. The detectives positioned themselves on both sides of him and escorted him out to their car. He was taken down to the station and questioned. Marcus would not admit to anything and they had no concrete evidence to charge him. They put him in a cell and went up to the hospital to question Felicia. They had to give her a pen and pad so that she could answer their questions. They found out that she did not see the intruder's faces and that she only heard a voice that sounded like Marcus.

They knew that without more than that they had no case. They were going to try to hold Marcus for seventy two hours to see if forensics could come up with some evidence that would link Marcus to the crime.

After being placed into a holding cell, Marcus called Karen. She answered the phone and accepted the call.

"They got you huh?" Marcus was taken aback by her comment. He was calling her to tell her that he was in jail and needed a lawyer and there it was she was acting like she was glad that he was in jail.

"What the hell is your problem Karen?"

"You dirty mother fucker! What you thought that I wouldn't find out?"

"Find out what?"

"That you were fucking my sister! Not just that, you tried to kill her. I hope that you rot in jail mother fucker!" Marcus regretted the fact that he did not make sure that Felicia was dead. He wished that he had shot her in the head instead of the face. He knew that she did not see his face, so he was going to deny it 'til the end.

"Karen, I don't know what the hell you are talking about. I wasn't fucking Felicia and I damn sure ain't try to kill her. What you are saying is crazy!"

"Save that shit for the jury nigga!" Marcus was getting upset, but he knew that he had to keep his cool. He needed to get that money out of her basement so that he could make bond once they charged him.

"Karen, look I'm going to send my cousin Eric over there to get a bag out of the basement. The key to the lock is in the kitchen drawer."

"Nigga! Ricky came and got that money."

"What!"

"You heard me! Ricky came over here and got that money. He described the bag before he even seen it. You're done!" Marcus knew then that it was going to be all bad. Felicia lived, Ricky got his money back and Karen had found out that he was fucking Felicia. He felt defeated. Karen was still yelling into the phone, when he hung it up. He went and flopped down on his bunk, trying to figure out how he could get up out of that jam.

π

Ricky went down to King Kennedy looking for Shotgun. He found him in front of Pack a Sack's store. He told Shotgun that he needed another gun, and Shotgun asked him what type he needed. He told him, "One that shoots a lot of bullets."

They got into Ricky's car and he drove around to Bundy drive. They entered building B15 and headed up to the second floor. Shotgun put a key into an apartment door and they entered. He led Ricky down a hallway to a backroom. He unlocked the door, opened it and they stepped in. Ricky was amazed. He just stood and stared at all of the guns that lined the walls, floors and stands that were in the room.

"Look around and see what you need." Shotgun told him. Ricky did not even know where to begin. He did not even know what he was up against. He still did not believe that Rocko could have done something to his sister. He knew that if he confronted him and things did not go right that he needed to be prepared.

He picked out a Uzi submachine gun and a 9mm with an extended clip. He paid Shotgun, then left. He drove down to Longwood to Rita's parking lot. He seen that Rocko's car was in the parking lot, then pulled over across the street to a payphone and paged Rocko. He waited for ten minutes before the phone rang. He picked it up and a voice on the other end asked, "Who is this?"

"It's Ricky man."

"Oh, what's up Ricky, long time no hear from."

"Yeah, I been going through some things."

"1 heard what happened my nigga. You have my sincerest condolences. You find out who did it and want to handle it in the streets, I'm with you. Whoever did that shouldn't be walking these streets."

"I appreciate all that you are saying, good looking."

"What's good though?"

"I'm trying to get a whole one."

"Damn my nigga, it is going to be a minute. I'm not in Cleveland right now. I'm on the freeway coming back from the D. Page me in about two hours and I should be up there."

"Yeah okay," Ricky told him then hung up. He wondered why Rocko would lie to him about his whereabouts. He decided to go and talk to Micky's mother. He drove over there and knocked on the door. Micky's mother opened the door and looked as if she had been crying for a week straight.

"Ms. Morgan, how are you doing?"

"I'm not doing too good, come on in." Ricky entered the house and she shut the door. You are Terresa's brother aren't you?"

"Yes ma'am."

"Hopefully they are together."

"What are you talking about Ms. Morgan?"

"Terresa and Micky, hopefully they are together up in heaven."

"What happened to Micky?"

"They found her in the graveyard behind King Kennedy. Someone had given her rat poison." she told Ricky then broke down crying again. Ricky did not know what to do. He did not know if he should try to comfort her or to just stand there and watch her cry. He decided to approach her. He wrapped his arms around her and let her cry on his shoulder. He knew the type of pain that she was feeling.

He was starting to believe what Coo Coo had told him more and more. He thought that maybe he should have found her some place safe to stay. He was then hoping that she was somewhere safe and that nothing had happened to her. He wondered if he should just go to the police or go confront Rocko. He decided not to do either of them. He decided to call his Pops, because he knew that his father would know how to handle it. He left Ms. Morgan's house and went to a payphone and called his parent's house. He got the answering machine. He tried two more times, then decided to leave a message.

On his parent's answering machine he left his father a message, "Pops, I think I know who killed Terresa. I need to talk to you." He hung up the phone and got back into his car. He drove back down to Longwood and parked across the street from Rita's parking lot.

He sat there for over an hour until he seen Rocko and two other guys leave out of the building and get into his car. Rocko pulled out of the lot and Ricky pulled off following him. He tried to stay at a safe distance, so that Rocko would not know that he was following.

Rocko drove as if he did not know that he was being followed, but he seen Ricky's car pull out behind him as soon as he pulled out of Rita's parking lot. He decided to take him to join Coo Coo. He drove back across 40th and down towards the abandoned factories. When he got down the hill he turned into the same lot that he had left Coo Coo in. When he pulled into the back of the building, Tookie got out of the car with a gun in his hand. He circled around the building and seen Ricky parked across the street with his eyes glued on the lot. He crotched down and crossed to the other side of the street. He stayed kneeling down, and was creeping towards Ricky's car, when a car started coming down the hill. Tookie did not want to look suspicious, so he stood up hiding the gun behind his back. As the car drove past Ricky he looked into his review mirror and seen a figure rise up. Ricky quickly opened his car door, jumped out and started firing his gun.

Him and the figure started firing at each other at the same time. It was like a shootout at the Okay Coral. They both stood shooting at each other without anything shielding them from the opposing gun fire. Ricky was hit first. He was hit twice in his shoulder and once in his chest. As Ricky was falling to the ground, one of his bullets hit Tookie in his throat. Tookie dropped his gun and put both of his hands up to his throat as he fell to the ground choking to death on his own blood.

Rocko heard the shooting when it started, but he hesitated before he decided to pull around to see what was going on. By the time he did pull around, both Ricky and Tookie were lying on the ground. Rocko pulled out of the lot and sped away.

Another passerby noticed two men lying in the streets and notified authorities. The police and the paramedics arrived onto the scene simultaneously. The paramedics found that Tookie was beyond helping. He was already dead. Ricky on the other hand was still alive and they started tending to him.

The detectives found, a firearm next to both of their bodies. They searched Ricky's car and found a UZI machine gun.

"Looks like this fella was ready to go to war." one of the officers said to his partner. The officers were told to canvas the area, and one of them noticed tire tracks in the gravel that were leading into the parking lot of the factory. Four officers followed the tracks around to the back of the building. They came upon a gruesome site. There lying on the ground was a young girl that they discovered had been shot in the head multiple times.

"Do you think that these crimes could he connected?" one detective asked the other.

"This body looks still fresh and whatever happened up there just happened. I think this is the third girl that has been found dead.

Mackie and Roberts need to be contacted. This could be connected to the case that they are working on."

Mackie and Roberts were called to the scene. When they arrived the channel 8 news was there and one of their correspondents was standing in the middle of the factory's parking lot getting ready to give a live report. Mackie and Roberts went to investigate the scene where the young girl was found, while the reporter started reporting.

"This is Martha Simmons from channel 8 news and I am here reporting live from the scene where two separate incidents have occurred. The Cleveland police department was notified about an hour ago that two men were lying in the middle of the street. Upon police arriving on the scene they did indeed discover two bodies lying in the street. One was dead and the other was transported to Charity hospital with life threatening gunshot wounds. A search of the area led police to another body. That of a young girl, which was located behind this building behind me. The girl was found to have been shot in the head a number of times. At this time police do not know if the murder of the girl and the shooting of the two men are related. The police are seeking help in identifying the young girl, whose picture will appear on the screen in a few seconds. Anyone with information as to who this young, teenage girl is please contact the Cleveland police department at 555-2123. Please stay tuned after the break, we are going to try to interview one of the detectives involved in the case."

They went to commercial. Mackie and Roberts were walking back from the scene where the girl was found. They had concluded from   the twisted angle that the girl's body was in, that she had been killed somewhere else and that her body was dumped there.

"I bet you that this one has to be the a friend of the other two." Mackie said to Roberts.

"It definitely seems like there is a connection. Whoever this bastard is, he doesn't deserve to be tried in the court of law. He needs to be hanged out in public!" Roberts said to Mackie.

"Do we have the names of the two guys that were laid out?" Mackie asked.

"Only one of them had identification on him. Get this his name is Ricky Henderson, which is the same last name of the first girl that was murdered."

"Is he the one that is DOA, or the one that survived?"

"He is the one that survived, and they also found an UZI submachine gun in his car."

"Let's run a check to see if he is related to the first dead girl. They were walking heading back towards their car, when they were called over by the reporter. The reporter told them that she would like to interview one of them on camera. She said that they could send out a plea for someone to come forward with any information that they might have regarding the incidents. Mackie told Roberts, "You go ahead. You look better on camera, than I do."

"Yeah, whatever!" Roberts said as he adjusted his tie and got ready for the camera. The technician signaled that they were getting ready to go back live.

"Three ... Two ... One." he counted down.

"This is Martha Simmons reporting live from the scene where two separate violent incidents took place. I am standing here with a detective from Cleveland's homicide unit. Detective Roberts could you tell us are these two incidents related?"

"We have not found anything that would suggest that they are just yet, but we are seeking help from the public in helping us identify the girl who was murdered. Anyone out there with any information regarding the identity of the girl or any of these matters please contact us."

"Okay everyone that was detective Roberts from the Cleveland homicide unit asking for your help in solving these tragic cases. The unidentified girl's picture is about to appear on your screen. Please contact the police if you know her identity."

19

Judy was at home in her room and had just turned on her television in time to see Coo Coo's face appear on the screen. "Oh, my God!" she said while staring at the television. She turned the volume up and listened to the reporter talk. The reporter mentioned that Coo Coo was the third girl that they had found dead in two weeks. Pictures of the other two dead girls were flashed on the screen. Judy looked at the screen and seen the faces of her three friends. All three of her friends were dead. She had just seen Coo Coo earlier that day. She started thinking about all of the things that Coo Coo had told her, and started to feel bad. She was starting to feel guilty, feeling that had she believed what Coo Coo was saying that she would still be alive. She was trying to figure out what it was that she should do.

She picked up the phone and dialed the number that was on the bottom of the screen. A police dispatcher answered the phone, and Judy told the dispatcher, "The name of the girl that they are showing on TV name is Carol Madden."

The dispatcher tried to get more information out of Judy. She tried to ask Judy her name and how she knew the victim. Judy was contemplating whether or not to give her anymore information or to just hang up. Judy was quiet and the dispatcher thought that she had hung up. "Ma'am hello?" the dispatcher said into the phone. All of a sudden Judy heard a knock at the door. She quickly hung up the phone and headed for the door. She went to the door, opened it and found Terresa's father standing at the door.

"We need to talk!" he told her as he stepped in and closed the door behind him.

"I think you know why I'm here. I need you to tell me who the guys are that Terresa and Micky were involved with." Judy broke down crying, "I did not know, I swear! I should have believed Coo Coo."

"You should of believed Coo Coo about what?"

"Coo Coo came over here earlier trying to tell me that Rocko had killed Terresa and Mickey, but I wouldn't believe her. Now she is dead too."

"How do you know that she is dead?"

"They just flashed her picture on the news. They found her down behind a abandoned factory on the other side of 40th and Woodland."

"Who is this Rocko and where can he be found at?"

"He is from Detroit, but he be on 33rd over this lady name Rita's house."

"Grab your coat, I need you to show me exactly where you are talking about."

"Aren't you going to call the police?"

"This can be handled without them." Judy got her coat and they headed out to his car. Harry drove around to 33rd and pulled into Rita's parking lot, "She stay on the third floor in the apartment on the left." Harry got out of the car and entered the building. He went up to the third floor and began knocking on the door on the left. No one answered the door, so he placed his ear to the door trying to hear if there were any movements or sounds being made inside. When he was satisfied that no one was there, he went back down to the car. He got into the car and asked Judy, "What type of car does Rocko drive?"

"He drives a black Maxima."

"How many guys do he be having with him?"

"At least three."

"Judy I'm about to take you back home, but I need you to do me an important favor."

"What's that?"

"I need you to forget that you ever saw me. We never had this conversation, and you can not tell anyone the things that you have told me. Can you do that for me?"

"Yes, I can do it." Harry drove Judy back home, then headed to the gun shop down on Broadway. He went into the gun shop and bought two .45 automatics along with two boxes of bullets. Then drove heading home.

π

The dispatcher had notified Mackie and Roberts of the call that she got giving the girl's name. They found out the girl's address and went to notify her parents of her death.

They arrived at Coo Coo's mother's house and gave her the devastating news. Coo Coo's mother broke down crying.

Once she got herself together she told the detectives the names of all of her daughter's friends. Mackie and Roberts felt the case breaking open when she told them, that her daughter hung with the two other girls. It was one other girl that she told them that her daughter frequently hung out with. They knew that they were going to have to track that girl down, but first they were heading to the Henderson's house.

When Harry got home and entered his house, he found that there were two detectives inside. They were talking to his wife. Harry tried to hide the bag with the guns in it behind his back. His wife was crying and both detectives were looking at him funny, because they seen the obvious move that he had just did.

"They shot him Harry! They shot Ricky!" Marlene told him crying.

"Who shot Ricky? he asked turning to the detectives.

"It seems that he was in a shootout at close range with someone else. We don't know how many persons were involved, but there was another guy found at the scene with him. That person is dead, but your son is at Charity hospital. Right now he is in surgery for a punctured lung."

"Good God, at least he is alive."

"Yes, he is alive. The doctors gave him a 80% chance of making it. Mr. Henderson, not far from where your son was shot a little girl was found murdered. We found out that this little girl was a friend of your daughter. The girl's name was Carol Madden, and after talking to her mother we found out that, she use to frequently hang out with your daughter. She even indicated that you knew that her daughter was a friend of your daughter. The last time we interviewed you, you informed us that you did not know of any other girls that your daughter was a friend of. Now we have found another dead girl, that was a friend of your daughter. It's apparent that all of your daughter's friends may be in trouble. We need your assistance in finding the bastard that is killing these young girls."

"I'm sorry, but I can not help you detective. As I told yon before, I do not know any other girls that were friends of my daughter. The only one that I remember is the one that you showed me in the picture."

"Well another thing that we are trying to figure out, is if your son could have possibly been doing some of his own investigating regarding your daughter's death?"

"Ricky has been going through his own problems as of lately. He did not have any time or know how to be investigating his sister's death."

"The whole situation seems strange Mr. Henderson and we are just trying to make sense of it." Mackie told him.

"Are you guys close to catching whoever is responsible for my daughter's death?"

"We are still searching for clues Mr. Henderson."

"Okay well, if you would excuse us, me and my wife would like to go up to the hospital and see our son."

"I must advise you that once your son is released from the hospital that he is going to be arrested. He may be possibly be facing a murder charge."

"Thank you for informing us," he told them as he escorted them to the door. After they were gone he headed upstairs to Ricky's room. He turned when he got to the top of the steps and told Marlene, "Get your things and go get into the car."

Harry went into Ricky's room and sat on his bed. He dumped the guns and bullets out of the bag. He opened up a box of bullets, took the clips out of the guns and started loading them with ammunition. Once he had both of the clips loaded, he put them back into the guns.

He stuck the guns into his waist, put the bullets back into the bag and left out of Ricky's room carrying the bag of bullets.

He called out to Marlene, and found that she had already left the house. He went out to the car and got in. Marlene was sitting in the car with her purse in her lap. Harry started the car and took off driving, heading up to Charity hospital.

When they got up to the hospital, Ricky was out of surgery. They had him in intensive care. They had Ricky in a room that had a big glass window that allowed you to look inside of the room. There was a police officer sitting in a chair outside of the room.

They were not allowed inside of the room and could only look through the window at Ricky.

Harry stood there staring at his son lying up there fighting for his life. He started getting flashbacks of Ricky and Terresa when they were kids. He remembered how they use to be happy kids. He could not figure out where it had all started going wrong. He had lost his daughter, now he was on the verge of losing his son. He stood there feeling like a failure. He thought that the only way he could be forgiven by his kids was if he could get justice, for them.

Marlene snapped him out of his thoughts. She started telling him how the day that she had bailed Ricky out of jail, that they had went up to the hospital to visit his girlfriend. She told Harry that she think the girl wrote down on paper the name of the person that had shot her. She told him that Ricky took off out of the hospital room as if he was going to seek revenge on someone. She told Harry, how Ricky would not even acknowledge her when she called after him.

Harry asked her did she see the name that the girl had written on the paper and she told him no. He asked her what Felicia's last name was and she told him.

He turned to Marlene and told her, "I have to fix this?" Marlene thought that Harry was losing his mind.

"Harry you do not have to fix anything. You let the police deal with this,"

"They are my kids Marlene. I was supposed to protect them. As their father, I must seek justice for them. I love you Marlene." he told her as he approached her and pulled her into his arms. Marlene wrapped her arms around him and squeezed him tightly. She cried in his chest, and they hugged for what seemed like eternity. Marlene did not want to let him go. Harry was giving her a scary feeling inside. To her it seemed like he was crumbling emotionally inside.

Harry forced Marlene's arms from around him. He held them together in front of her, and kissed her on top of her forehead. He let go of her arms and turned heading down the hall. She called after him.

"Harry! Harry please come back!" she stood there crying. It was like dejavu all over for her, as she stood and watched Harry storm out of the hospital. Harry jumped into his car leaving one hospital heading to another. He drove up to Kaiser Hospital and went up to Felicia's room. Felicia remembered him from the funeral and knew that he was Ricky's father.

Harry approached the bed, "I need your help? I need the name of the person that Ricky went after. Ricky has been shot and that person may have had something to do with it."

Harry handed Felicia a pen and a piece of paper, and she wrote a name down. She handed the paper back to Harry and he looked at it.

"Do you have a address for him?" he asked her. She shook her head and he handed her the paper back. She wrote down her sister's address and handed it back to him. He folded the paper up and stuck it into his pocket. He told her, "If you need anything you just contact my wife. You are carrying my grandchild, which makes you family. You and your child will never want for anything."

He bent over and kissed Felicia on her forehead, then left her room. He pulled the paper out of his pocket that she had written on. He looked at the address on it as he walked to his car.

20

Forensics could not come up with any evidence that would link Marcus to the crime, so the detectives were forced to let him go.

They released Marcus and he called Karen trying to get her to come and pick up, because he had no money on him. Karen picked up the phone and when she heard his voice she hung it up. Marcus got mad and thought about how he couldn't wait to get to her. She did not know that he was free. He couldn't wait to see the fear in her face, when she seen that he was out.

He found a driver that took sympathy to the fact that he was on crutches and gave him a ride to Karen's house.

The driver dropped him off in front of the house and he climbed out and used his crutches to hop up onto the porch. He knocked on the door to gain entry, because Ricky had taken his keys. Karen went to the door and asked, "Who is it?"

"It's me! Open the door."

"Your not coming in here Marcus, just leave!" Marcus got mad and started beating on the door with one of the crutches, "Bitch! I'm going to fuck you up if you don't open this door."

Karen went to the window and pulled the curtain back. Marcus walked over to the window and began cursing at her through it. He did not even notice, when Karen's eyes grew wide. She was looking past him to the big man that was walking up on her porch. She stood there and watched in horror as the man raised two guns and started unloading them inside of Marcus' body. Blood flew out of Marcus' mouth onto the window as she stood in it.

The man stood over Marcus and fired his guns until there were no more bullets in them. Both guns were smoking in his hands. He made eye contact with Karen then calmly walked off of her porch. Karen ran to the phone and called 911.

The man got into his car, reached into the backseat and grabbed the bag that held the bullets. He sat there in front of Karen's house and reloaded the guns, then took off heading down to Longwood.

π

Detectives Roberts and Mackie were heading down to investigate a potential lead. The call that had come in identifying the girl had been traced. A check of the address revealed the name of the other young girl that was known to hang out with the three victims.

They were two blocks away, when they received a call from dispatch instructing them that they were needed at another murder scene. The dispatcher gave them the address, and they made an uturn heading to the address.

"Fuck! We can't get a chance to solve one murder before another pops up!" Mackie said out loud.

"They got rabbit season, duck season and now it seems as if they got human being season." Roberts said to him.

"People sure are starting to think that they have to kill. It's our job to put a stop to it."

"Isn't it crazy how we have to do our job backwards?" Roberts asked Mackie.

"What do you mean?"

"Well our job is supposed to be to serve and protect right?"

"Yeah so,"

"Think about it, how often do we prevent murders from occurring? We are usually called after the murder has already occurred."

"Yeah, I see what you are saying. That's our job as homicide detectives to solve the crimes."

"Yeah, but who is responsible for preventing them?"

"It is impossible to prevent all crimes from happening. There are not enough police officers in the world to do that." Mackie told Roberts as they pulled up to the scene.

When they pulled up, there were police everywhere. Spectators lined the sidewalks and stood on porches watching as the body was being put onto a gurney.

Two other detectives were questioning the lady that stayed at the residence. Roberts and Mackie approached them and Roberts spoke, "Michaels and Smith what do we have here?"

Michaels answered him, "Seems like we have an execution style murder. The victim was shot thirty two times." Mackie responded.

"Yeah, whoever done it had to be really angry. This was over-kill."

"So, what do you have so far?" Mackie asked.

"This here is Karen and the vic was her ex-boyfriend. He was trying to get her to let him inside of the house, when somebody walked up onto her porch and began filling him with holes."

"What do you guys know about the victim?" Roberts asked them.

"We know a lot about the victim. We just released him this morning." Mackie told them.

"What were you holding him for?"

"Suspicion of aggravated robbery and attempted murder." Michaels reached into his pocket, pulled out a notepad and flipped it open.

"The case was crazy. The victim's name is Marcus Ware and he was accused of breaking into his girlfriend here, sister's house and shooting her. We questioned the sister's boyfriend at the hospital and he gave us permission to go and search the house for evidence. During a search of the house, we found some dope and a firearm. We went back to the hospital and arrested the boyfriend. We concluded that he was a drug dealer and that it was a robbery that had taken place. The sister did not see the face of the intruders, and forensics couldn't connect Ware to the crime, so we had to let him go this morning."

"What was the boyfriend's name?" Mackie asked.

Michaels flipped the page over in the pad and said, "Ricky Henderson."

"Ricky Henderson?" Mackie asked again in disbelief.

"I know, it's getting crazier and crazier," Roberts said to Mackie.

"What you guys know something that we don't?" Michaels asked them.

Roberts turned to Karen, "Ms. Harrison, can you describe the man that came up onto your porch and shot Mr. Ware?" Karen gave them a description and both Mackie and Roberts shook their head. They came to the same conclusion.

"Mr. Henderson!" Mackie said to Roberts then took off heading to their car. Roberts took off behind him, leaving Smith and Michaels standing looking dumbfounded.

They jumped into their car with Roberts driving. He was heading up to Charity hospital and while they were driving he asked Roberts, "Do you think that he is seeking revenge for his kids?"

"1 don't know, but if he is, we better hope that he doesn't find the person that killed his daughter. Thirty two bullets is overkill."

"I don't know about Ware, but whoever killed those young girls needs to be killed a hundred times over."

"That may be the case, but that is not our job. Our job is to find and apprehend the culprit." Roberts pulled into the hospital's parking lot and they exited the car. They went into the hospital and up to the intensive care ward. They found Mrs. Henderson talking to one of the doctors, getting an update on her son's condition. They interrupted her and the doctor, telling her that it was important they talk to her. Mackie asked her, "Mrs. Henderson where is your husband?"

"I have no idea."

"You do not know where your husband is at?"

"No, he left a little while ago."

"Mrs. Henderson, do you think that your husband is out trying to take justice into his own hands?"

"Harry would not dare do such a thing."

"We would like to believe that also, but some events that have taken place are suggesting otherwise. The man that allegedly shot your son's girlfriend was just murdered. He was shot thirty two times, and the witness gave a description that fits your husband."

"Marlene's heart dropped inside of her chest. There was no doubt in her mind that Harry was the one that killed that man, but she knew that she could not let the detectives know that.

"There must be some type of mistake, Harry would not shoot anyone, let alone kill someone."

"We really hope that is true, Mrs. Henderson, but as of right now we need to locate your husband to ask him a few questions."

"Well as I said I have no idea where he is. When I hear from him, I will be sure to have him contact you."

Mackie and Roberts were both frustrated, but they knew that there wasn't anything that they could do. If her husband was guilty, she made it apparent that she was not giving him up.

They were leaving the hospital, heading to their car, when Roberts asked Mackie, "Can you blame her?"

"Can I blame her for what?"

"For protecting her husband,"

"In a sick twisted way, no I can't. A dead daughter, a son clinging to life. She probably thinks that what her husband did was justice."

"We have to find him before he administers anymore justice."

"The only way that we are going to find him is to find the killer of his daughter. That has to be his next target." Roberts told Mackie.

"I say let's go and interview the remaining girl. I think that is our best chance." Mackie replied.

"Say no more, that is where we are headed."

21

Harry was parked in Rita's parking lot. It was starting to get dark outside, when he seen two women walk up. He took in the women's appearance and thought to himself, "They must be crack heads." He watched them head towards the building that he had been staking out. He got out of his car, adjusted his guns, then headed to the building. When he entered, the two women were heading up the stairs. Harry looked up, watching the ladies climbing the stairs. He slowly crept up the stairs behind them. Once they reached the third floor, he got a feeling that one of the women were Rita. He seen them turn to the door that he had knocked on earlier and one of the women put a key in the door and opened it.

When they closed the door behind them, Harry hurried up the stairs. He put his ear to the door trying to hear what was going on inside. Through the thick door, he could only make out muffled sounds.

He pulled out one of his guns, put it down to his side then knocked on the door. Rita and Pam were at her kitchen table. They had just copped a twenty and were about to get high, "Somebody is always trying to fuck up a bitch trying to get high." Rita said as she got up from the table and went to answer the door.

"Hopefully it's that nigga Rocko. I got a few words for him." Pam said out loud. Rita went to the door and opened it. Her face turned into a mask of horror, when she came face to face with a big gun pointed at her face. She looked at the face of the man that held the gun. He had a finger up to his lips, indicating for her to be quiet.

He put the gun on the tip of her nose and started walking forward. Rita started walking backwards, and once the man was inside of the house, he closed the door behind him.

Pam realized how quiet it had gotten and called out, "Who is it Rita?" When Rita did not answer, she got up from the table and walked to the living room. When she got there, she seen Rita sitting on the couch looking like she was scared to death.

''Bitch what's wrong with you?'' she asked her. Harry came up behind Pam and put the gun in her back.

"What the …" Pam began while turning around. She never got to finish her sentence. The big gun pointed at her face silenced her instantly.

"Go sit next to your friend," Harry told her. Pam walked over to the couch and sat down next to Rita. Harry stood in front of the two women and began talking.

"Look you two have nothing to worry about as long as you do what I say. Which one of you are Rita?" Pam quickly pointed to Rita, "She is!" Rita looked at her like she wanted to kill her.

"Okay Rita, here's what I need you to do. I need you to get in touch with Rocko and get him down here." Rita looked at him then said, "You want to rob Rocko?"

"No, I want to kill Rocko, the same way that he killed my little girl!"

"Whose father are you?"

"I'm Terresa's father."

"Oh shit!" Pam said.

"I haven't seen Rocko and I do not know when he will come down here."

"I'm going to be honest with you Rita. If you want to live you will find a way to get him down here. This here is not a game and there will be no negotiating. It's either his life or both of your lives, you choose."

"Rita! Bitch! Stop playing with that man. Page Rocko's shiesty ass!" Rita became so scared that she could not control her bowels. She got up shaking like a leaf and headed to the phone, which was on the kitchen wall. When she walked past Harry, he held his nose and asked her, "What did she do," and she replied, "I'm sorry but you scared the shit out of me!" Pam wanted to laugh badly but knew that it was not the time.

"Rita girl, you done shit your pants. You never could hold your mud." Harry gave Pam a crazed looked and she instantly got quiet. Rita paged Rocko and stood by the wall, but Harry got tired of smelling shit and told her to go take a seat back on the couch. Rita went back over to the couch and sat down, smashing the shit onto her ass cheeks.

They waited tor about fifteen minutes before the phone rang. Harry instructed Rita to go answer it, and she did.

"What up?" Rocko asked her.

"When are you coming down?"

"Why?"

"Because I got somebody that's trying to spend some money."

"Rita, I ain't coming down there for no fucking twenty dollar sale!"

"No, this dude got real money and is trying to get something big."

"Look, I'm going to send Marco down there. If shit ain't right I'm going to fuck you up Rita!"

"Dude would rather deal with you!" she told him.

"Why the fuck do it matter who he deals with. Tell him he deals with Marco or he can push on." Rita covered the phone and told Harry, "He said that he ain't coming, that he is sending his dude."

"Tell him to send him!" Harry whispered to her.

"Okay Rocko, he said send him."

"Ask him what he wants?" Rita knew that Harry did not know anything about no dope, so she just made up something.

"He said he wants a eighth."

"Tell him that Marco will be there in about twenty minutes."

"Okay," Rita told him then hung up.

"Can I go clean myself up now?" She asked Harry.

"You go ahead, but if you try anything funny, I'm going to kill you and your friend. Do you understand?"

"Perfectly!" she answered as she headed down the hall with the back of her pants sagging.

π

Mackie and Roberts were at the Weakley's residence. They were sitting in the living room talking to Judy parents, who were trying to get a full understanding of the situation.

"So, you say a call from this house was traced, and that someone called from here and identified a dead girl?" Judy's father asked.

"Yes sir," answered Mackie.

"May I ask the names of the girl?"

"Actually, Mr. Weakley three girls have been murdered and they all were friends of your daughter Judy."

"What are their names?" he asked again. Mackie gave him the names.

"God Darryl, those are the girls that we told Judy to stay away from."

"Detectives I doubt that my daughter has any information that will help you. She hasn't been allowed to be around those girls for some time now. We have always known that those girls were trouble." Roberts spoke, "They might have been trouble Mr. Weakley, but surely they did not deserve to be murdered. Your daughter may possess some information that could help us find these girls' killer. We would appreciate if you would let us talk to your daughter."

"Let them talk to her Darryl, that is the least we can do."

"Judy get in here!" her father yelled. Judy came out of her bedroom and entered the living room. She saw the two detectives and knew what they were there for.

"These are policemen and they said that you made a call to them earlier about one of those girls that we told you to stay away from. Did you call them?"

"Yeah, I called them. I seen Coo Coo's face on the news and they were trying to identify her. I called and gave them her name."

"These gentlemen would like to ask you some questions, that they think may help them catch the girl's killer."

"Judy, my name is detective Roberts and we are investigating the death of your friends. We need to know if you have any information that could help us find their killer. Do you know of anyone that would want to hurt them?"

"No, I do not."

"When was the last time that you seen or talked to any of the girls?"

"It's been months."

"Think deeply for a minute, and see if there is anything that you may have forgotten, that may help us." All Judy kept thinking about was her promise to Terresa's father. She felt that she had let Coo Coo down and she did not want to let Mr. Henderson down.

"No, I haven't forgotten anything. I'm sorry that I can not help you."

"That's okay," Roberts said to her. He turned to her parents, "Thank you for your time."

"No problem officer." Judy's father told them as he led them to the door. As soon as the officers left Judy broke down crying, "What's wrong?" her mother asked her.

"Nothing!" Judy said then ran back into her room. When her father came back into the living room, her mother told him, "I think she is holding something back. I'm going in her room to talk to her." she got up off of the couch and headed into Judy's room.

π

Thirty minutes had past and still no one had showed up at Rita's. Harry was starting to think that no one was coming. Rita and Pam, were nervously sitting on the couch. Rita had washed and changed clothes.

Finally, there was a knock at the door. Harry indicated for Rita to go to it. He positioned himself behind the door and gave her the okay to open it. She opened the door and Marco walked in. As soon as he was inside of the door Harry clobbered him over the head with one of the forty fives. Marco went crumbling to the ground, but Harry wouldn't let him hit the floor. He grabbed him by his collar to prevent him from falling and hit him upside the head with the pistol again. After the second blow he allowed him to crash to the ground. He pulled out the other forty five and pointed both guns at his face, "Here is the choice that you have Marco. You can take me to Rocko or you can die right here. Which one will you choose?"

Marco took too long answer and a gun went off. Both Rita and Pam jumped in fear, while Marco cried out in pain.

"Listen carefully that was my daughter that Rocko killed! Somebody has to pay for her death. It's either Rocko or you. Now let's try this again. I know that you are in pain, so if you decide that you want to live shake your head indicating that you are going to take me to Rocko." Marco quickly shook his head.

He had no part in the girl's death, and did not want to die behind something that Rocko done.

"You aren't going to kill us are you?" Pam asked him.

"Go and get something to wrap his leg in." He said to Rita. Rita went and tore a towel and brought it back to him. He told her, "Tie it around his leg" Rita walked over to Marco who was sitting up on the floor and tied the towel around his leg. Harry reached into his pocket and pulled out a knot of money and threw it to Pam. Rita seen what he had done and dove through the air tackling Pam.

"Bitch! We in my house that's my money." The two of them were wrestling on the floor, when Harry escorted Marco limping out to his car at gunpoint.

"What car are you driving?" Harry asked Marco and he pointed to it. They headed to that car with Harry getting into the passenger's side. Marco complained that he could not drive with the pain in his leg. Harry told him that he only needed one leg to drive, so he better use his good leg. He rode with his gun pointed at Marco as he drove.

22

After talking to Judy, her mother called the number on the card that the detectives had left them. Judy had confessed to her that she had lied to the detectives. She told her mother about her conversation with Coo Coo and about the visit that Mr. Henderson had paid her.

"You talked to that poor girl only hours before she was killed?" her mother asked her.

"I did not believe that Rocko could do something like that."

"So, you know this guy Rocko?"

"Yes,"

"Why didn't you tell the detectives Judy?"

"Because I promised Mr. Henderson that I wouldn't."

"Terresa's father does not know what he is getting involved in. This character sounds real dangerous, I'm calling the detectives back over here and you tell them everything that you know about this Rocko fella, you hear me?"

"Yes,"

Mackie and Roberts came back to the house and listened to all that the young girl had to tell them. Mackie asked her, "So you seen Coo Coo hours before she was killed and she told you that Rocko had killed Terresa and Micky and was trying to kill her?"

"Yes sir!"

"But you did not believe her?"

"I use to talk to Rocko and did not think that he was capable of doing such a thing."

"Explain what she said happened to Terresa." Judy told them the story that Coo Coo had given her about what had taken place at Rita's house.

"And you told that story to Mr. Henderson?"

"Yes,"

"You took Mr. Henderson to this Rita person's house?"

"Yes,"

"And what happened?"

"He went and knocked on her door, but wasn't anyone home."

"He brought you home, then what happened?"

"He had me promise that I would not tell anybody about our conversation."

"Do you have the address for Rita?"

"No, but I can show you where she lives." Roberts looked to her parents to see what their reaction would be.

"I'll get my coat." Judy's father told them. He grabbed his coat and his wife grabbed her purse and they all headed out of the door.

Judy rode in the back of the car with the detectives. She gave them directions, while her parents trailed behind them. When they got to Rita's parking lot, she pointed out the apartment building to them. Mackie noticed that it was a car sitting in the parking lot that fit the description of Mr. Henderson. Judy told them that the apartment was on the left side, on the third floor.

The detectives thanked her and let her rejoin her parents. She got into the car with them and they headed back home.

Mackie and Roberts got out of their car.

"That looks like his car over there." Mackie said to Roberts. They walked over to it and flashed a flashlight inside of it.

"There on the floor," Roberts said to Mackie. They both observed what looked to be a bag of bullets lying on the floor in the back seat.

"I think we need to call backup." Mackie said to him.

"We may need a SWAT team Mr. Henderson isn't in the right state of mind at this moment." They went back to their car and radioed in for a tactical team to come to the scene.

π

Marco pulled up into the driveway and cut the car off. Harry got out of the car and went around and helped Marco get out of the car. Once Marco was out of the car he helped him up the steps. When they got up on the porch.

Harry told Marco, "What happens from this point on determines whether you live or not. You get Rocko to open the door, without trying anything funny and you get to walk away from here alive, you got that?" Marco shook his head indicating that he understood.

"Go ahead and knock on the door." Harry positioned himself on the side of the door, where he could not be seen. Marco knocked on the door and a voice asked, "Who is it?"

"It's me nigga!" Marco replied.

"It took you long enough!" Rocko was saying as he opened the door. Soon as the door opened, Harry quickly stepped from his position and hit Rocko on the top of his head with his gun. One blow would not take Rocko down. The blow stung him, but as Harry tried to hit him with another blow Rocko rushed at him. Rocko was just as big as Harry and he rushed him with so much force that they both went tumbling down the steps. Marco took off limping inside of the house.

He was not taking any chances and was going to arm himself. Harry and Rocko tumbled down the stairs, and Harry lost his grip on his gun as he fell. When they hit the ground they tussled with each other.

Each one trying to get loose to get to the gun. Rocko was younger and stronger than Harry and he over powered him. He got on top of Harry and pounded him in the face and once he thought that Harry was out of it he got up and went for the gun to finish him off.

His back was to Harry when he went for the gun, so he did not see Harry pull the other .45 from his waist. Harry waited for Rocko to pick up the gun, and as soon as he turned around Harry started unloading in him. Harry heard a shot that did not come from his gun and a chunk of gravel hit him in the face. He rolled over onto his back and started shooting at Marco, who was firing at him from the porch. Two bullets hit Marco in the face and he went down.

Harry stood up, walked over to Rocko's body and emptied the rest of his clip into him, "That's for my baby girl!" he said to the dead man.

Harry pried the gun out of Rocko's hand, went up onto the porch and into Marco's pocket. He took the car keys out of his pocket, got into the car and drove off.

π

A tactical unit arrived down in Longwood. Mackie and Roberts advised them of the situation, they told them that it may be a hostile situation in an apartment on the third floor of the apartment building.

He told them that they needed the tactical team to breach the door for them. Roberts and Mackie both put on bulletproof vest, so that they could go in with the team.

When everyone was in place the team went into action. They headed upstairs, with the first two officers carrying a battering ram. The second two officers carried a shield and cans of tear gas.

They approached the door and the lead man raised his hand, ready to give the signal. He knocked on the door.

"Police! Open up!" Rita started choking on the smoke that she had taken in from the crack pipe. Her and Pam had taken some of the money that they had gotten from Harry and went and bought themselves a eight ball of crack. There was dope all over the table and they both had crack pipes.

They had no intentions of getting rid of the dope, so they started stuffing it wherever they could.

Because they did not answer the police demand for entry, the officers breached the door and rushed into the house with their firearms at ready. Some turned their guns on Rita and Pam, while others went to check the other areas inside of the apartment.

Rita started howling, because she had stuck the hot pipe inside of her bra and it was burning a hole in her breast. Pam was high and could not respond to the officers demands for her to get onto the floor. The officers rushed her and threw her down on the floor and cuffed her. Rita was screaming, "I need a doctor!" They threw her onto the floor and cuffed her too.

After they searched the apartment and found it to be clear, they sat Rita and Pam on the couch.

"Do y'all have a warrant? We ain't got no drugs in here!" Mackie spoke, "This isn't about no drugs, it's about murder!"

"Shit, we ain't killed nobody!"

"No, but Rocko has."

"I don't know any damn Rocko."

"Listen we can do this here or we can do this downtown. We know that you know that Rocko killed those young girls, and we know that this man came here looking for him." Mackie showed her and Pam a picture. They looked at it and recognized the man as the one that took Marco.

That man was out to avenge his daughter. He is a good man and had given them a lot of money. There was no way that they were going to give him up.

"Look, we know Rocko, but we don't know what he did or did not do. We never witnessed anything, and I have never seen that man in that picture in my life. Now if you are going to arrest me because I don't know anything, then you go right ahead."

"Where does Rocko stay?" Mackie asked her.

"I have no idea, whenever I want him I have to page him and wait for him to call me back."

"We need you to page him."

"I'm kind of tied up at the moment." Rita said to him being funny. Mackie uncuffed her and allowed her to page Rocko. She paged Rocko three different times and he never called back.

A uniformed officer came into the apartment and told Mackie, "We just got a call that two men were killed out in Maple Heights, not more than an hour ago. One of the men had a Detroit driver's license that listed the name Roger Moore."

"I don't see how you can get Rocko from Roger, but that has got to be him."

"What's the address?" The officer gave them the address and they headed out there. There wasn't anymore need for the tactical unit, so they headed back to the department.

π

Harry drove down to the flats and threw the guns into the water. He parked the car that he was driving in a downtown parking lot and wiped it clean of his prints. He caught the bus back up to Longwood.

He got off at 30th and Community College. He walked up to 33rd to Rita's parking lot. His car was still parked there. He waited for about twenty minutes, looking for any sign of the police's presence. After he felt it was safe, he went and got into his car and pulled off. He was heading home when he realized that he still had the bullets on the back floor, he pulled into a parking lot that held a green dumpster and threw the bag of bullets into it then he headed home.

π

Mackie and Roberts arrived at the scene out in Maple Hts. There was a man shot twice in the face lying on the porch, and a man lying dead in the driveway was shot fourteen times.

"At least he got it less than Ware did." Roberts said.

"I wonder does this bring the saga to an end?" Mackie stated.

"Well, it's time to pay another visit to the Henderson's home. Now that his mission is completed, where else is it for him to go?" They got into their car and headed back to the Henderson's residence.

Harry arrived home and found Marlene sitting on the living room sofa in the dark. When the door opened Marlene jumped up. She gave a smile that could light up the night, as she ran to him. She threw her arms around him.

"Harry, thank God you're alive. You must go! We have to hide you!"

"Hide me, why Marlene?"

"The cops they are looking for you. They are going to arrest you for murder."

"We have nothing to worry about Marlene. Everything is going to work out fine. You grab your purse, and we can go down to the station. I'm going to turn myself in and let things work themselves out."

"They could give you the death penalty Harry. Don't turn yourself in."

"Marlene you have faith in God don't you?"

"Yes I do,"

"Well, put your trust in God that things are going to work out." Marlene grabbed her purse and they left heading to the police station.

23

Mackie and Roberts arrived at the Henderson's residence and found that there wasn't anybody at the house, "You think they could have skipped town?" Mackie asked Roberts.

"With their son in the hospital fighting for his life, my guess is that the mother would stay. Maybe she took the father to catch a plane or a train, but I doubt that she would leave her son."

"Well, let's go back to the station and contact all the airlines, bus and train stations to see if he took flight." Mackie told him.

They headed back to the station. When they got there, they were informed by the desk sergeant that there was a Harry Henderson that had walked into the station saying that he was turning himself in for questioning.

"Where is he?" Mackie asked the sergeant.

"He is in one of the interview rooms and his wife is sitting in the hall." he told him.

Mackie and Roberts took off to the interview room. When they turned down the hall they saw Mrs. Henderson sitting on a bench. As they approached, she stood up.

"How are you?" Roberts asked her.

"Harry has come to clear his name. I knew that he did not do what he was accused of."

"Let us be the ones to figure that out Mrs. Henderson." Mackie told her as he headed into the interview room, with Roberts following behind him.

They entered the room and Harry was sitting in a chair as if he did not have a care in the world. Roberts closed the door and stood against it, while Mackie pulled up a chair and took a seat.

"You know that you are in some serious trouble Mr. Henderson?" Mackie said to him.

"That remains to be seen." Harry responded.

"We know the whole story about your daughter and son. We have witnesses against you. You can give us your side of the story and because of the extenuating circumstances we may be able to get the prosecutor to offer you a deal."

"If you are going to arrest me, I would like to call my lawyer."

"You will be allowed to call him once you have been booked into the county jail." Mackie told him.

"What is it that I am being charged with?"

"Three counts of aggravated murder." Roberts told him as he pulled out his cuffs and approached Harry.

"Mr. Henderson could you please stand up and put your hands behind your back." Harry stood up and placed his hands behind his back and Roberts cuffed him and began reading him his rights.

They led Harry out of the interview room. Marlene seen them bring Harry out in cuffs and jumped up off of the bench.

"What are you doing, he hasn't done anything?"

"Mrs. Henderson, your husband is being arrested on three counts of aggravated murder." Mackie told her.

"Marlene don't worry just call our attorney. Everything is going to work out fine." he told her as they led him away in cuffs.

π

The next day all the news stations ran the story all day. They reported that the father of a slain daughter and a son that was in the hospital fighting for his life after being shot, decided to take the law into his own hands. They also reported that there were witnesses linking Harry to the murders of the alleged assailants of his children.

People started getting riled up, and choosing sides. Some took in the fact that three innocent young girls were killed and thought that what had been done to the suspects was justice and not murder.

The prosecutor was out to make a name for himself during election time and attached the death penalty to the charges. He told the public, that the state of Ohio was not going to accept people acting as vigilantes and that people who decided to take the law into their own hands were going to be prosecuted to the fullest extent of the law.

The judge set a trial date for Harry, who had no intentions of pleading out anyway. He felt that he did what he had to do for his children and if God wanted to punish him by putting him to death or having him spend the rest of his life in jail, then so be it.

He hired the best attorney that he could, Henry Mancino. Mancino had a family ran practice that consisted of his son and wife. Henry Mancino knew that he was going to need a whole team to help him fight the case against Harry. Truthfully he thought that what Harry was doing was suicidal.

He thought that the cards were stacked against Harry. He had two witnesses against him, one that witnessed him kill a man on her porch.

Harry had decided not to pursue a plea bargain and as his attorney his job was to represent him to the best of his ability and that is what he planned to do.

The prosecutor knew that he had a airtight case and could not wait to grand stand in front of the jury.

π

On the opening day of the trial, the court room was packed. There was no where to sit and people stood outside of the courthouse carrying picket signs that read: "Free Harry Henderson."

Some carried signs that said: "It was justice not murder." Both sides picked the jury, then opening statements began. The prosecutor told the jury that he had two witnesses that would prove that Harry Henderson had killed Marcus Ware, Roger Moore and Marcel Whittikar.

The prosecutor first called the detectives to the stand, so that they could paint the picture for the jury as to what led up to the murders.

Everything was going good for the prosecutor until his star witnesses got on the stand.

First he had Judy on the stand. He questioned her about the things that she had told the detectives about Harry Henderson. For some reason she did not remember telling the detectives anything about Mr. Henderson. She admitted that she had made the call about Coo Coo. She told him that she did tell them that Coo Coo had told her that Rocko killed Teressa and Micky. She stated that she never seen Mr. Henderson.

"Ms. Weakley are you going to sit up here in front of this jury after being sworn in, and tell us that you did not see Mr. Henderson on the day of the murders?"

"I did not see him."

"Did you talk to him?"

"No, I did not."

"Could you explain to us, why you told the detectives that you did?"

"I told them what they wanted me to tell them. I just wanted them to leave me alone. I had lost three of my friends and was scared. They were pressuring me." Mackie and Roberts looked at the girl in disbelief. They could not understand why she had gotten up on the stand and started telling lies.

The prosecutor got frustrated and ended the questioning. The court gave the defense an opportunity to cross examine her and the defense refused.

Next the prosecutor called Karen Harrison to the stand. He knew that with her testimony that he was sure to get a conviction. Everything was going good until the prosecutor asked her was the person that shot the man on her porch in the court room. To that question she answered, "No,"

A loud roar went through the courtroom. The prosecutor was flabbergasted. The whole case had started to crumble right before his eyes. He was determined to get a conviction and started treating Karen as if she was a hostile witness.

"Ms. Harrison isn't it a fact that on August 14th, Mr. Henderson shot and killed Marcus Ware on your porch as you watched through the window."

"Marcus was shot, but not by the person who is on trial."

"You did not identify Mr. Henderson as the killer to the detectives?"

"They asked me for a description and I gave them one. They never showed me a picture of that man. Had they, I would have told them that he was younger than him and a lot darker."

"Your honor, may I approach the bench?" The prosecutor asked. The spectators in the courtroom, felt like the prosecutor was about to try and pull a trick to keep from cutting an innocent man loose. They started chanting, "He's not guilty! He's not guilty!"

The judge banged her gavel, "Order in the court, order in the court! I'm giving you all a warning anymore outburst such as the one that just happened and I will clear this courtroom." everyone settled down and the judge spoke.

''You may approach the bench Mr. Franklin. Defense counsel rushed to join the prosecutor at the bench. The judge turned on the white noise box, so that no one in the court room could hear what was being said at the side bar.

"Your honor, I know for a fact that those two witnesses committed perjury on the stand."

"If that is true, then prosecute them. Do you have anymore witnesses to call?"

"No I do not, but I would like to request a recess until tomorrow morning, so that I can get to the bottom of why my witnesses all of a sudden changed their stories."

"I would like to object to that your honor. I think that the government was given a sufficient amount of time to prepare and present his witnesses. I request that we continue with the trial and also. I would like to make known that at the conclusion of the trial, I will be making a motion for judgment of acquittal due to lack of evidence."

"It is noted Mr. Mancino. First off I sustain your objection to the government's request for a recess. The government was given sufficient time to prep his witnesses. I will tell you now that I am denying your motion for acquittal. If both sides find that they have no more witnesses to present, we will have a half an hour recess and then present closing arguments."

"I have no more witnesses your honor." the prosecutor told her.

"Neither do I." Mancino responded.

"Okay, we will recess for a half an hour then start closing arguments. The prosecutor and Mancino returned to their benches and the judge turned off the white noise. She told the court room, "We will be recessing for thirty minutes, and then we will start closing arguments."

Everybody started filing out of the courtroom. The prosecutor shot over to Mackie and Roberts.

"My God, what happened with those two? Did someone threaten them or something?

"I don't think that is it. I think they see him as being a hero!" Mackie told him.

"Hero my ass! That man is an animal. He killed three people in cold blood. If he walks I am going to prosecute both of them for perjury!" Roberts thought to himself, "Would he really pursue charges against a sixteen year old girl?"

After the recess was over, closing arguments were had. After the prosecutor finished, the judge sent the case to the jury.

The courtroom stayed packed and people lined the walls, waiting for the jury to return a verdict. Some people in the courtroom felt that if Harry did kill those men, that, it was justice and not murder.

The jury deliberated for one hour and came back with a verdict. The court's clerk informed the judge that the jury had reached a verdict and the judge called the court back into session.

Marlene was sitting in the first row, right behind Harry, with her fingers crossed. The jury's foreman stood up and read the verdict, "We the jury finds Harry Henderson not guilty on all charges."

The court room went crazy. Everyone was yelling and screaming. The judge banged her gavel trying to restore order, but no one was paying her any attention. They started chanting, "Harry! Harry! Harry!" Marlene ran around to Harry's table and wrapped her arms around him. Harry hugged her back, while his attorney stood looking shocked.

They had seen many things happen inside of a courtroom, since they had been lawyers, but the things that took place in Harry's trial amazed them.

The judge had security to start clearing the courtroom. Harry was a free man and he and Marlene walked out of the courtroom walking hand in hand.

When they got outside of the courthouse there were television cameras everywhere. All the reporters were fighting to get an interview from Harry. When Harry was about to climb into his attorney's car, one got close enough to stick a microphone in front of Harry's face.

"Mr. Henderson how do you feel?"

"Like justice has been served." Harry told him then climbed into the car.

Epilogue

Ricky claimed that the shooting was in self-defense and there was no evidence or no one to dispute it. Ricky's name was not on the lease and he never admitted that the gun or the drugs were his, so those charges were dismissed also.

When he was released, he and Felicia got married. They had a little boy and named him after Ricky's father. Ricky did not sale anymore drugs, instead he took a job at the steel mill with his father.

New Flavor Books

New Flavor Books & Publishing LLC
Book Order form

Full Name: _____

Institution# (If applicable):_____

Address: _____

Address 2: _____

City:_____ State:_____ Zip:_____

Book Title:	Price/Quantity
Hood to Hood: A Cleveland Story	*$15.99* _____
Hood to Hood 2: Spank's Revenge	*$15.99* _____
Sexual Addiction: Director's Cut	*$15.99* _____
All Flavors: A Book of Erotic Short Stories	*$9.99* _____
Bisexual Bliss	*$15.99* _____
Murder or Justice	*$15.99* _____
Hittin' Licks	*$15.99* _____
Total Including ($3.00) Shipping and Handling	_____

To place an order for one of our books please send a payment
for the price of the book plus $3.00 for shipping and handling to:

New Flavor Books & Publishing, LLC

C/O Book orders

P.O. Box 603323

Cleveland, Ohio 44103

Please allow 2 - 4 weeks

New Flavor Books

D M Gaines

www.ingramcontent.com/pod-product-compliance
Lightning Source LLC
Chambersburg PA
CBHW072136170626
46813CB00004BA/1589